Ivan's Choice

Also by Kathy Clark

A Whisper In My Heart

Guardian Angel House

The Choice

IVAN'S CHOICE

Kathy Clark

"It takes courage to grow up and
become who you really are."

e.e cummings

Prologue

Two wars raged during the fall of 1944. One was fought in the world around me. The other was fought within the battlefields of my own heart and mind. I was thirteen years old. Eager to face the danger of combat in the streets. Confident of my physical strength to overcome the enemy. But the conflict within my soul terrified me. Losing some part of myself was inevitable.

Wars don't start all of a sudden. There is a long period of conflict between opposing sides - a buildup of tension; of uncertainty about if and when to take decisive action. The official start of World War II was September 1st, 1939 when Hitler's Nazi army invaded Poland.

The start of my personal war came much later. It was on Sat. Nov. 5th 1944. But, as with all wars, it too was preceded by a period of conflict, tension and uncertainty. Still, I was unprepared for the decisive action I chose to take that day. My personal declaration of war.

Kathy Clark

Chapter 1

Sat. Nov.5, 1944; 7am. Budapest, Hungary

I studied my reflection in the mirror with a mixture of pride and trepidation. Today, wearing this uniform that Father had borrowed for me, I would look like a true soldier. One of the many who were engaged in fighting this war on behalf of our country. This was not the childish uniform of my Levente youth group, the military group that all boys over the age of twelve were required join. Today I would easily pass for the young man that I aspired to be. Over the summer months I had grown and my shoulders had broadened so that the uniform jacket did not sag as I had feared it would. Today I would be one of the Arrow Cross. Just like Father.

My bedroom door opened. "Looks great!" Father said. He smiled and winked at my reflection. "I'm glad to see you're ready. We'll be leaving in a few minutes." I tensed at his words, then let out a sigh of relief when he hurried away. I wished that I could feel as confident inside as I looked on the outside.

Father was looking forward to me seeing firsthand what his new job as an Arrow Cross sergeant entailed. He was as keen as I was that I make a good impression on the soldiers under his command. I wanted to live up to his expectations, to suppress my growing unease about the methods that the German Nazis and the Arrow Cross used to keep the Jewish population under control. An unease that thus far, fearing his wrath, I had carefully hidden from Father. As I turned away from the mirror and went to follow Father, I promised myself that today I would strive to see things through his eyes. That I would make my father proud of me!

Ever since the Nazi German occupation of Hungary on March 19th, 1944, the plight of the Jews had drastically worsened throughout the country. Especially here, in its capital city, Budapest.

"All Jews must wear a yellow star on their outer clothing! Jews can no longer own property!" Father had read the rules out loudly from the morning newspaper two days after the Nazis arrived. "Jews may not be actors, lawyers or bankers. They may not have any government jobs. They are not permitted to own vehicles! They may not ride bicycles!" Father's eyes shone with satisfaction.

"At last something is being done to control and hopefully to rid this country of its vermin!" he said.

By October, in order to help them carry out their mission, the Nazis reinstated the previously outlawed Arrow Cross party as the head of the government. Father, who had secretly been an Arrow Cross member for years, was promoted to the prominent rank of Captain.

Under his authority, the ghetto was created. It was an area within the heart of Budapest that walled in several blocks of apartment buildings and shops and where most of the Jews of the city were forced to move.

It was this ghetto that was our destination today.

We would inspect it and round up the Nazi's daily quota of Jews to be shipped to labour camps. Since I would see a large number of Jewish people together in the ghetto, I hoped to prove to myself that Father, the Arrow Cross, the Nazis and all the people who supported them, were indeed right in their condemnation of the Jews.

Chapter 2

Sat. Nov.5, 1944; 3pm

"Go! Run!" My father spit the words at me. His face was flushed. Though I knew that I was not the cause of his anger, an icy fear gripped my heart and froze my feet to the pavement. People's lives depended on what I was about to do.

"Alert the guards on our street!" Father yelled. "The whole Varga family must be rounded up at once, including their servant. Go! My chauffeur will drive you back. I can't spare any of the men here. The guards will trust you," he said, as if reasoning with himself. "They'll do as you say. They know you are my son."

I stole a quick glance at my best friend Hendrik Varga who had so unexpectedly materialized in the doorway of the apartment building we were about to enter and who was the cause of this present turmoil.

I was desperate to ask him what he was doing here in the ghetto. How, when did he get in? And why he was saying that his name isn't Hendrik? That it's Jakob? That he is a Jew? But in front of Father, in the midst of the commotion, I was powerless to speak. And when Hendrik looked back at me, his expression was defiant. Shutting me out.

*****

Nothing about this trip to the ghetto had turned out as I had hoped. My expectations of the day crumbled within minutes of stepping through the gates.

The ghetto was located on the Pest side of the Danube River. It was near the heart of the city – an area of several intersecting streets that had been segregated from the rest of Budapest by a large stone wall. Most of the Jews from the city and surrounding area were forced to move there. Others lived in the designated 'Jewish' buildings nearby. The two gateways into the ghetto were heavily guarded by a combination of Arrow Cross and

Nazi soldiers. They monitored both the people and the supplies going in and out.

I was surprised to see the number of people living inside the ghetto walls. People milled about aimlessly in the streets and sat on the building steps. Yet, every apartment Father and I entered was crowded with several families squeezed into a space intended for only one. In many, the smell of unwashed bodies, garbage and sewage permeated the air. It bothered me to see people living in these conditions. I couldn't help but compare this to what now seemed as our own luxurious apartment where I had a large bedroom all to myself.

Though I hadn't really thought about it, I had assumed that only adults would be confined to the ghetto. I was disturbed at the sight of numerous disheveled children milling around the adults Everyone in the streets, including the children, had the required yellow star stitched to their outer garments identifying them as Jews. Rounding one corner, I was shocked to see Mr. Weiser the tailor, his shoulders hunched, among them. The last time I saw Mr. Weiser he was fit and his regular, jovial self. Now he looked shrunken and miserable. Why was he in here? Surely *he* wasn't a threat to the country!

I had been wondering when Mother and I would visit Mr. Weiser again. Over the summer months I had rapidly outgrown the brown woolen suit he last sewed for me. I needed to get measured so that my next suit would be ready in time for Christmas. Now I realized that Mother had probably been trying to find a new tailor. I would not be returning to Mr. Weiser's shop.

I tugged at Father's sleeve to ask if a mistake had been made, but the steely glare of his eyes silenced me. Father too had recognized Mr. Weiser yet seemed to accept his presence here as nothing unusual. Father's expression commanded me to do the same. I reminded myself that today I intended to see everything through Father's eyes. I straightened my shoulders and tried my best to reflect Father's confidence. To copy the enthusiasm and determination of the other Arrow Cross soldiers as they carried out their duties. There had to be a good reason for what I saw around me. For why the Jews, including Mr. Weiser, were being treated this way. The problem had to be with me.

But no matter how hard I tried, I couldn't stop the feeling of shame that enveloped me. I turned my eyes away from Mr. Weiser. I had always liked him. He spoke to me as he would to an adult and whenever we left, he always tucked a candy into my palm when we shook hands. I wondered if he had recognized me. If he had seen me wearing the Arrow Cross uniform. It was a shock to admit to myself that I hoped not. Much had changed since I looked at myself in the mirror just hours ago.

As we marched from one cheerless street to another, I recognized a few other familiar faces. My cousin Adelle's piano teacher, the dentist who had let me push the button that made his chair go up and down when I was six and the girl, my age who had lived just a few blocks from us and who had rushed to wipe the mud from my skin and clothes when I crashed my bike in front of her building. All these people, just like Mr. Weiser, seemed like shrunken shadows of their former selves.

Father called the Jews in the ghetto 'vermin' or 'dogs'. "We move them to the ghetto so that they can no longer contaminate the rest of us," he had explained on our ride over. "Also this way, it's easier collect the ones that will be sent to the camps. You'll see."

Though I saw, I couldn't see it the way Father did. *'Aren't they people just like us?'* Hendrik's question kept intruding itself into my mind. I had thought that the Jews in the ghetto would be more like criminals. Villains who were destroying our country as the billboards suggested. But these were ordinary people I had played with and learned from. People who used to be my friends. I had hoped that today would settle the conflicting thoughts and feelings inside me and I would march proudly at Father's side. That wasn't happening.

The soldiers under Father's command looked at him with respect as they hurried to obey his orders. I wanted to do the same but found it more and more difficult to do so. The Arrow Cross had a long list of people to round up that day and Father instructed me to help them.

"Make sure the younger children stay with their mothers! Don't let anyone get out of line!" he said. The soldiers hauled people from their apartments into the street. Once everyone was assembled they would be marched off to the Western Railway Station and then carted off to who knew where. An army truck followed slowly beside us onto which soldiers forced the more difficult people. Armed guards were in the back of the truck with them.

Fearing to disobey Father, I pretended to be pleased at being put to work.

"Go on! Get moving! We haven't got all day!" I yelled at a poor woman who was desperately grabbing at small items to stuff in the pockets of her coat before stumbling down the stairs to join the others. I helped herd the frightened people from one bleak street to another, though I refrained from prodding and pushing them as the soldiers did. I waved my club above their heads but was careful to never actually hit anyone. Whenever I got close to a child, I whispered a couple of words of encouragement in their ear so that they would hurry along and avoid the wrath of the officers. Apart from quickening their steps for a few paces, I doubted that my words did much good to calm them. My uniform identified me as one of the people to be feared and despised.

As the day wore on, despite not actually hurting anyone, the shame of my involvement with the Arrow Cross grew. I cringed inwardly whenever Father or one of the soldiers praised what I was doing. I wished that I had never come to the ghetto with Father. I wished that I could go back to not fully knowing or understanding what was happening here. I wished that I hadn't seen Father at work and could continue to admire everything about him as I had before this day.

And then, just as we were preparing to enter another dismal apartment building, its large metal doors burst open and there stood Hendrik.

Chapter 3

Hendrik stood wide eyed, his arms gripped firmly by two soldiers. A third one had a gun pointed at his head.

"Why Hendrik, whatever are *you* doing here?" Father had asked when Hendrik first burst out through the building's gate. There was a moment of silence during which Hendrik's expression rapidly transformed from surprise to fear to one of defiance. He pulled himself up straight, raised his hands and pushed against Father's chest.

"I'm not Hendrik," he said. "I am Jakob. Jakob Kohn. And I am a Jew!"

For an instant all the air seemed to be sucked out from the space around me. What was Hendrik saying? What did this mean? Was it true? I felt lightheaded. This was my friend. My best friend! A Jew?

And he was confronting Father! Father who did not tolerate opposition from anyone.

Several things happened at once. One of Father's men grabbed Hendrik by the shoulders while another stepped up and slapped him hard across the face.

"What do you mean by pushing an officer?" He demanded. Blood ran from Hendrik's nose down to his chin. I winced at his pain. The soldier holding Hendrik shoved him to the ground and pointed a gun at his head. I was too shocked to utter a sound. Where I stood, slightly behind Father, Hendrik had not yet noticed me.

A woman, who had appeared in the doorway behind Hendrik, screamed when Hendrik collapsed to his knees. A young girl around twelve, who stood next to her, started to cry.

"Wait," Father shouted to the guard, and held up his hand to stop any further abuse. He turned back to Hendrik.

"What is this about Hendrik?" he asked. "Or is it Jakob now? What are you saying? What kind of tricks has your family been playing with us? With my Ivan?"

I cringed at Father's last words. At Father's tone of voice. I could sense his rising anger. I too was staggered by Hendrik's admission. Yet I could understand, after all that I had witnessed this morning, why he and his family, if they were indeed Jewish, would want to hide that fact from us.

Especially us, with my father an Arrow Cross Commander living right across the courtyard from them!

Suddenly, Hendrik's questions, his scruples over the past several months about how the Jews were being treated made sense. He was the one who had first nudged my own conscience, who had opened my eyes to the reality of what was taking place in the city around us. Who had first made me question the posters with their warnings about the Jews.

If I had been more willing to listen, to understand, if I hadn't always started my response with "but Father says…"; if I hadn't resorted to Father's authority, would Hendrik have trusted me more? Had he been trying to, wanting to tell me all along?

What I couldn't understand was why Hendrik had revealed his family's secret now – to Father – and why he had decided to come to such a horrid place as this ghetto.

But there was no time for speculation.

"Yes, yes. I see that you are telling me the truth now," Father was saying. "You and your parents had dared to lie to us. To me! To my son! You will *all* suffer for this!" Father's voice escalated with each sentence till he was shouting at Hendrik.

"What else could we do but lie?" Hendrik shouted back.

I trembled with fear on Hendrik's behalf. 'Please don't yell at Father,' I pleaded silently, 'you will just make things worse'. Unaware of my presence and mute entreaty, Hendrik continued with a raised voice.

"We had no choice. It's because of people like you. Why are you doing this to us? Jews are just like everyone else. You know our family. You know me." Yes! I silently applauded his words. I wanted to punch my fist high in the air, impressed with Hendrik's sudden courage to stand up to my father. Courage that I lacked.

"Take him away," Father barked at the guards. "Arrest these people associated with him and take them too." He gestured towards the woman and girl still standing horror-stricken in the doorway. "*Jakob* will learn what we do with liars. He will learn never to deceive anyone again."

It was just as Father had finished giving this last order that a young man who looked to be in his mid to late teens, came around the corner.

"Mother! Lilly!" he shouted as he swiftly took in the scene and saw the soldiers reach for the woman and girl. He ran towards them at full speed.

"Ah, another one," Father sounded pleased. "Take him as well!" he ordered.

The soldiers dragged and pushed the woman and girl onto the back of the nearby truck at gun point, while others grabbed the young man's arms. Enraged, he yanked one arm free and grabbed the barrel of the gun pointed at the woman, veering it away from her. In the same instant the soldier standing next to Father aimed his gun at the young man's chest and fired. The man's body crumpled into a motionless heap on the ground. A pool of red blood oozed from beneath him. The woman screamed again and lunged from the truck. The guards caught her in mid stride and held her back.

It was as Hendrik was being forced towards the truck at gunpoint that Father turned and yelled for me.

"Ivan! Hurry home and alert the patrols on our street!"

I stepped out from the shadows behind him.

Hendrik paused. He turned in my direction. He noticed my presence for the first time. For a split second our eyes locked. I hoped that my eyes said what my lips could not: "I understand! I understand everything now. I'm sorry."

But Hendrik stared back at me. The look in his eyes was one of disgust as they travelled down the length of my body, not seeing me, his friend, but my uniform and what it represented. Then the moment was gone. Hendrik looked away and with head held high, climbed into the truck.

Chapter 4

"Go!" my father yelled at me again. "What are you waiting for? They mustn't find out what happened here and get away. They must pay for their deceit; for making fools of our family like this! Go!" My gaze flicked from Hendrik back to my father.

"Yes Sir!" I shouted back. I had to obey Father. No one dared to question his authority. I stood at attention and gave a quick salute, just as I had seen the other Arrow Cross officers do.

It was only after I had started to run towards the gates of the ghetto, towards Father's waiting car with its chauffeur, that the full impact of what had happened and what I was about to do, hit me. My best friend had just been arrested. I was about to assist in condemning his family to the same fate. Was that what I wanted to do? Did I really have to obey Father?

My steps slowed.

I remembered what Brother Ferenc had said in last week's religion class when he explained that we would begin our preparation for the sacrament of confirmation.

"Confirmation is your gateway to manhood," he said, looking intently at each one of us. "At your confirmation, you will accept responsibility for your own religious formation." His eyes, his words, seemed to bore into my soul. "When you were a child, your parents made the decision for you. Until now, the responsibility to raise you in the faith was theirs. Now, when you are confirmed, the choice will be yours."

Hendrik and I shared a desk and we had exchanged a quick smile. We agreed with Brother Ferenc, understanding that his words applied to all areas of life. Over the summer months we had taken on the responsibility of shaping our bodies as quickly as possible to become those of young men. We exercised, willingly undertook any physical work, built up our muscles. Now Brother Ferenc was saying that we were ready to form our minds and hearts as well. To develop our consciences.

It was Brother Ferenc's words that had inspired me to decide once and for all, whether or not I agreed with Father and the ideals of the Arrow Cross and Nazis.

Was it those same words, I wondered now, that had also led Hendrik to the ghetto today? If he and his family were indeed Jewish, but had been living as Catholics for years, did he too want to see, to decide for himself which religion he wanted to be a part of?

Confirmation was a big step. Brother Ferenc had made that clear. Was Hendrik in the ghetto trying to decide which path to follow?

Judging by what he said to Father, he had made his choice.

Now, I had to make mine.

Chapter 5

Throughout the day as I helped to arrest and herd Jews into the street, I increasingly realized that my aim of seeing the Jews through father's eyes was not working. That it never would.

But I hadn't thought that I would have to do anything about it. I figured I could just go along as I had been. Silent. Keeping my thoughts to myself, my silence giving the impression that I agreed with Father. One time, when I had worked up the courage to question him about the treatment of the Jews, he had become very angry. He slammed his fist onto the arm of the easy chair he was sitting in.

"We should have gotten rid of them all, a long time ago!" he exclaimed. "We've been too weak! We've let them infiltrate all aspects of our lives and this is what comes of it! Cockroaches! All of them! Skittering everywhere they have no business to go!" Father jumped up from his chair and stretched, flexing his arms over his head. "I'm just glad that I'm finally in a position to do something about it!"

On another occasion, when I saw an elderly Jewish man being dragged along the street by his beard I couldn't stop myself from asking. "Is it necessary for the soldiers to be that cruel? He hadn't done anything wrong. He's just on his way to the store like we are."

"The soldiers are not being cruel!" Father said through clenched teeth. "They are treating him as he deserves. The Jews are worse than the pigs they won't eat." *I couldn't treat a pig or any animal that way,* I thought, and opened my mouth to say as much, but Father's next words silenced me again.

"It isn't those Franciscan Friars at your school putting strange ideas into your head, is it? Flowery notions of gentleness and peace? I'm not spending good money on a private school if they are going to corrupt you."

"No, no!" I hastened to reassure him. "I – I was just wondering. I'm sorry. I didn't mean to object." I liked the school I attended with Hendrik and my other friends. I liked the quiet sense of wisdom that seemed to permeate the very walls of the ancient building. I didn't want to say anything that might sway Father to choose a different school for me. It was better to just remain silent. It was not as if I could do anything to influence what was happening anyways.

But this time it was different. It wasn't just a matter of keeping silent. I was being ordered to do something. Something that would drastically affect the lives of my best friend and his family.

It would be so much easier to simply follow Father's orders, I told myself. That was my duty – to obey Father, whether I liked it or not. There was no risk involved in doing that. Father would be pleased that I had helped and would probably give me increased responsibilities in the Arrow Cross. My dream of becoming a soldier would be so much closer. I could ignore and maybe with time overcome my scruples about the Arrow Cross and the Nazis. I would rise in its ranks. Father and I would work side by side. As his son, I would be respected and admired along with him.

I was so lost in thought that I accidentally bumped into a man standing at the end of a short line, waiting to purchase some bread. He recoiled when he saw my uniform.

"I, I'm so sorry," he stammered. "I didn't see you sir. I didn't mean to be in your way."

"It's alright," I said, ashamed again that my uniform inspired such fear in a man older than Father. "It was…" I had no chance to finish my apology. A soldier who happened to be marching by saw the incident. He grabbed the man's coat collar and threw him to the ground.

"Stay out of our way pig!" he yelled. He winked at me and went on his way.

I wanted to rush to the fallen man's side, to help him up and brush the dirt from his coat. But my uniform and everything it represented, the other soldiers laughing nearby, prevented me from doing that. My shame turned to loathing. I wished that I could tear the uniform from my body.

No! I would have no part of this! I would not be responsible for the Varga family's arrest.

The image of Hendrik pushing against Father and yelling at him flashed in my mind. I recalled my feeling of triumph at Hendrik's courage to stand up to Father. It reignited my own. My limbs tingled with renewed energy.

I didn't have to obey Father. I must figure out a way to save Hendrik's family. To hide them and maybe even rescue Hendrik. But, if possible, without Father suspecting that I had anything to do with their sudden disappearance.

I started to run.

Chapter 6

I opened the door of the patrol car and collapsed onto the backseat. I closed my eyes and calmed my breathing.

"Please," I said to the driver once I had caught my breath, "take me back to my home. Father wants me to deliver a message." The driver nodded and turned the engine on. I tried to force myself to push the disturbing events and images of the past hour out of my mind and to focus instead on coming up with a plan to rescue the Vargas. But Hendrik's shocking confession, the look on his face when he saw me, refused to fade.

We had been the best of friends for years, ever since his family first moved into our building, right across the courtyard from our apartment. From that first day, as we climbed among the limbs of the majestic chestnut trees that lined our street, I knew that we would be inseparable. Scenes of Hendrik and I chasing through the cobble stone streets on our bikes, fishing on the banks of the Danube on lazy summer afternoons, creeping through the dark, forgotten and abandoned labyrinth of tunnels beneath the Buda hills, flashed through my mind.

As we grew, our childish games of pretense – of being pirates, hussars, villains and heroes alike, gradually transformed into the more mature ambition of becoming soldiers. Soldiers who would help to win this war to the glory of our country.

It was Hendrik who had planted the first seeds of doubt in my mind.

"I've been thinking, you know?" he had said one day in March, shortly after the German troops arrived in Budapest and all those edicts against them were printed in the newspaper. "There are two sides in every war. How do we know which is the right one?"

"Why, the one that is defending our country," I replied, taken aback by the oddity of his question. But then, Hendrik was always talking about strange things. I figured it was on account of all the books he read when we weren't out doing things together.

"Defending our country from whom? The Nazis?"

"Of course not!" I had said, shocked that he had dared to suggest such a thing. "Against the Jews of course. That's why Father and the Arrow Cross, why everyone is supporting the Nazis."

"But what's wrong with the Jews?" he had persisted. "There might be a few that aren't good. Just like with any group of people. Does that mean we need to restrain all of them? Rid the country of them?"

I had responded with Father's words that day. Referring to the Jews as thieves and cockroaches. I pointed to the posters plastered everywhere. Hendrik had just looked at me and sighed. Then he turned back to our dart throwing competition that his questions had interrupted.

But after that day, I started to notice things more. How people who were part of our community one day would be arrested the next because it was discovered that they were Jews. My doubts about the Nazis and Arrow Cross grew over the following weeks and months as I witnessed the increasing injustices and brutality in the city around me. But they were doubts that I never acknowledged to Hendrik because of my loyalty to and fear of Father.

Now I understood why Hendrik had asked those questions. I looked out the car window at the posters plastered on the news boards and sides of buildings. One showed a Jewish man running off with bags of Hungarian money. Another portrayed a Jew, whose face very much resembled that of a rat, dangling people like marionettes. I turned away with disgust. What had Hendrik felt when he saw those posters? Would things have turned out differently if I had confided my growing misgivings to him?

I shook my head. I must focus! I had to find a way to alert the Vargas of their impending danger and if possible, help them hide somewhere before I gave Father's orders to the guards patrolling the street. Father must believe that I fully obeyed him. The consequences otherwise were unthinkable.

I was thankful for the extra time that the car's slow progress along roads congested with both vehicles and horse-drawn carriages gave me to think. It would have been quicker to take the streetcar to the other side of the Danube and then the trolley up the mountainside to our tree lined street. Many of the buildings we passed here, were similar to the one my family and Hendrik's lived in. Ancient, re-purposed mansions, their massive ballrooms and libraries now divided up into individual apartments; the servant's quarters in the basement transformed into root cellars or storage areas for coal. It was in our own coal cellar that Hendrik and I had discovered the long-forgotten, subterranean passageway that connected our building to the one across the street and from there led to a little used alleyway. I wondered if there were such tunnels here, beneath these buildings built on the flat terrain of Pest as there were beneath the buildings scattered across the hills of Buda.

Suddenly I sat up straight. The tunnels! They were my solution! That's how I would get into the building undetected and back out onto the secluded alleyway with the Vargas!

Chapter 7

Hendrik and I hadn't visited the cellar in ages, but surely the passage was still there, and as unknown as ever to the rest of the world.

But what was I to do with the Vargas afterwards? I couldn't just abandon them in the alley. The soldiers would easily find them if they started searching the area.

I noticed that we were crossing the Danube River now, on Erzsebet Bridge. The water below swirled grey and cold reflecting the somber hue of the gathering clouds above. Soon we would be winding up the curving streets that led to our neighbourhood in the hills of Buda. The traffic there would be lighter and despite the steep, winding roads, we would travel at a faster pace.

We reached the other side and the driver turned left onto the ramparts towards the road that circled the base of Gellert Mountain. I still had no plan. If only there was someone who could help me. Someone I could trust. Someone to tell me what to do with the Vargas.

The road wound behind the steep hill. Across the valley, part way up the side of Sas Mountain, I could now see the spire of the Church of St. Francis poking up above the treetops. Though hidden from view, I knew it was flanked by the Franciscan Monastery on one side and the private boys' school that Hendrik and I attended on the other.

Each of the classes at the school, math, history, literature, was taught by one of the Franciscan friars. At first, Hendrik and I chuckled over their shaved heads ringed by a narrow band of hair, their coarse, brown, hooded robes. At times, I wondered why anyone would choose to live a life of such simplicity and poverty. But after years of study at the school, I was no longer distracted by their oddities. I had grown to respect the disciplined and challenging, yet always interesting lessons. And my favourite was always religion class, taught by Brother Ferenc.

Brother Ferenc! Would he help? He was the wisest person I knew. Several times in the past few months he had cautioned us not to believe all the propaganda that bombarded us over the radio, in the newspapers and on the billboards. He reminded us to always respect everyone's human dignity regardless of their race, religion or status in society. Surely, I could trust him. He would know what to do with the Vargas. But how could I reach him without my chauffeur knowing? Before even alerting the Vargas? Before relaying my message to the soldiers?

Just then, as if in answer to an unvoiced prayer, our way was barred. A long convoy of German army vehicles was slowly making its way up to the army base located in the Citadel on the top of Gellert Mountain. Who knew how long we would be stuck here in one place? This was the opportunity I needed.

"I can get out here," I leaned forward and said to the driver. "My father said I had to hurry to deliver his message. I know a short cut. I can get to our building faster on foot than sitting in this car."

"Are you sure?" The driver looked hesitant but sounded relieved. If I left, he could turn the car around and head back to the ghetto. I was sure that was where he preferred to be and he had no reason to be suspicious or to doubt my intention.

"Yes, I'll cut straight through there," I said pointing to a narrow, cobblestoned passageway between two buildings. "It connects to Meredek St. which is just blocks from where I have to go. And it's midafternoon already. By the time we would arrive back at the ghetto it would be almost time to come home anyways. You can tell my father that because of that I decided to stay at home and wait for him there."

"That's good thinking," the driver said after giving my plan a moment's consideration. "I'll tell your Father that you took the quickest route possible to deliver his message. You'll be a fine member of the Arrow Cross one day. Pretty soon, I assume," the driver added and winked at me. I nodded back with a forced smile and jumped out of the car.

Chapter 8

I started running as soon as my feet hit the pavement and within seconds, I disappeared into the shadows of the narrow passage. There were many of these old lanes interlaced throughout the city, a remnant of past decades and even centuries, when many of the apartment buildings were large mansions and these lanes led to stables or other outbuildings at the back of the property.

At the far end of the lane, I turned left and zigzagged my way towards Sas Mountain and up the hillside towards the Franciscan monastery. Though I was fit, by the time I arrived at the low wrought iron fence that circled the monastery grounds, I was out of breath and my legs were shaky. I was sure that I had covered the distance in record time. I pushed through the tall gates and hurried up the short path to the main building. I pulled on the bell rope beside the heavy, intricately carved wooden front door and heard the muffled metallic clanging on the other side of the thick stone wall. After a moment, a friar, whom I recognized but whose name I didn't know, slowly creaked the door open.

"I need to see Brother Ferenc," I panted, still trying to catch my breath. The friar stood there in his plain brown cassock, calmly studying me from head to foot. I had forgotten that I was wearing the Arrow Cross uniform. An Arrow Cross soldier at your door was always a concern these days, even if you were on their side.

"Please," I urged, "it's important!"

"Step inside and wait here," he said, then turned and silently shuffled down the marble floored corridor in his felt slippers and disappeared around a corner. I looked around me at the bare, grey stone walls and the large wooden beams supporting the high ceiling of the foyer. I had never been inside this side of the monastery before. There had been no need. Now I saw that the same simple grey stones and dark walnut beams had been used to construct this building and both the school and the church. I knew that the Franciscan brothers obeyed a vow of poverty and it was evident in the lack of ornaments or signs of comfort even in this, their home. The only object that adorned one of the side walls was a large crucifix. Against the opposite wall was a plain stone bench.

I didn't know how long I would have to wait. I thought of sitting down, but I was too restless. I needed to be out of here and on my way to alert the Vargas of their danger. But the plan was useless if I had no place to take them once I convinced them to flee. My only hope for now was in Brother Ferenc. That *he* would come up with a plan.

I thought of Jakob as I paced back and forth and wondered what was happening to him at this moment. If Father wanted his parents rounded up, it must mean that he intended to keep Jakob captive, at least for a while. Perhaps I should have said something in Jakob's defense before I left. But no. I reminded myself that when Father was enraged as he had been at discovering the Vargas' deception, anything anyone said to counter him would backfire. I was doing the only thing I could, the best I could do.

To my surprise, Brother Ferenc appeared within minutes, hurrying towards me. He was old. Well past sixty, I thought. Maybe even seventy.

From behind his ears, a narrow stubble of white hair circled his otherwise bald head. From his bearing you could tell that once his body had been powerful and strong, though now his brown hassock hung loosely around his shoulders. Still, he moved with great energy and his deep brown eyes were alert to everything going on around him.

"Why Ivan," he said when he recognized me, "I didn't realize that you had joined the Arrow Cross. Just like your father, I see." Did I detect a hint of disappointment in his voice? Right now, I was counting on that being the case.

"No, no," I hastened to reassure him, "Father just had an opportunity to take me along on his inspection rounds, and he thought it would be a special treat to get a uniform for me." I walked towards Brother Ferenc but stopped short of reaching him and lowered my gaze in shame.

"I, - I didn't know what it would be like," I stammered. "We - we went to the ghetto," Suddenly I was all choked up and tears sprang to my eyes. I was desperate not to cry. I wanted to act like a man. A man of confidence, strength and honour. The man brother Ferenc had challenged us to be.

Brother Ferenc laid his hands on my shoulders. "It's alright," he said, "I understand." And then he pulled me into an embrace. "It is good that you have compassion for those who are persecuted."

My relief at his understanding unleashed all my worries and fears, and I must admit that for a couple of minutes I could do nothing but cry. The images of the ghetto, the poverty, the trash in the streets, the illness and the desperation in people's eyes, and always my father's gloating over them, his commands, the beatings, the fear, the unjust power, and my complicity in the whole situation, washed over me. I felt a desperate need to be cleansed of the day's events and for the first time I longed for the sacrament of confession.

"But what brings you here? Why do you wish to see me?" Brother Ferenc asked, stepping back.

"It's Hendrik," I blurted out. "He was in the ghetto; I don't know why he was there. I don't understand. But Father found him and Hendrik said he is a Jew, and that his name is really Jakob, and Father's soldiers killed someone and I think that Hendrik," I shook my head, "no, I should call him Jakob now – that Jakob is being taken away and Father ordered me to come back and tell the guards on our street to round his family up. But," I stumbled over my words between sobs, "I can't do that. I can't obey Father. I have to help the Vargas somehow." I took a steadying breath. "I couldn't do anything to help Hendrik, or Jakob that is, in the ghetto. But I think I can help his parents get away before the guards come to arrest them. I just don't know what to do with them after that."

I leaned my head into Brother Ferenc's shoulder, relieved at having unloaded my burden onto him.

"Can you get Jakob's parents here?" he asked. "Without being seen by the guards?"

Chapter 9

I lifted my head and looked at Brother Ferenc with wonder. Was it going to be this simple?

"Yes. Yes. I can do that," I said. "But are you sure? I don't want to put you in danger."

"The urgent thing right now is to not let the Arrow Cross or the Nazis get at them. I've heard horrible rumors of what happens to the Jews that are arrested. There are many unused rooms here at the monastery. I will find one to hide the Vargas in until we can figure out something better."

"Thank you!" I said with heartfelt relief. "I had figured out how to get them out of the building and hide them in an underground tunnel. I was planning to go back and give Father's message to the guards in the street only after that. Then I was going to sneak back into the tunnel and take Jakob's parents somewhere. But I – I didn't know where. It would be only a matter of time before the guards discovered the tunnel if they were thorough in their search. The Vargas would be found. But if I could bring them here," my voice dropped. I still couldn't believe that Brother Ferenc truly meant what he said.

"Yes, yes. You must go at once," Brother Ferenc agreed, "But first," he laid a detaining hand on my shoulder, "for the first part of your mission, you should change out of that uniform. It makes you too conspicuous. You are less likely to be noticed if you enter and exit the building near your apartment as a regular civilian. Then, when the Vargas are safely gone, then you can change back into the uniform and alert the guards." I nodded my agreement glad that Brother Ferenc had thought of that detail.

He led me to a small room that opened off of the foyer and was filled with an assortment of large boxes. He opened the first one closest to us.

"These are donations for the poor in the community," Brother Ferenc explained as we rummaged through an assortment of pants and shirts and sweaters. I picked out items that I thought would fit me and help conceal who I was. A pair of brown pants, a nondescript grey sweater, a thin black jacket and a black cap that was too large, but which slid down over my ears and would hide my face. I thought of the people in the ghetto and hoped that one day soon I could smuggle some of these clothes to them.

Once I was dressed again as a civilian, Brother Ferenc bundled the Arrow Cross uniform into a brown paper bag and handed it to me.

"You had better take this with you to change back into, once Jakob's parents are on their way here," he said. "That will save your having to come all the way back here with them. You will be able to alert the guards on your street more promptly, causing less delay in carrying out your father's orders." I nodded in agreement. I was glad that Brother Ferenc had the foresight to consider that as well, and thankful that I had come to him for help.

In about ten minutes after arriving at the monastery, I was back out on the sidewalk in front of the wrought iron fence.

"I will pray for your success," Brother Ferenc said as he closed the gate behind me.

Chapter 10

I hurried towards our street, keeping my head down, holding the paper bag under my arm and willing myself not to attract attention by running. When I got close, I circled around a couple of blocks and entered through the front doors of the building that backed onto ours. Because a shoe repair store and a tailor were located on the ground floor of its courtyard, the large front doors were kept unlocked during the daily business hours. Keeping to the side of the courtyard, I made my way to the dark opening of the back stairway and rapidly descended the ancient stone steps.

There were no lamps here to light my way and I was upset at myself for not bringing a flashlight or some matches and a candle. Still, the subterranean walkways were not totally dark. Dim rays of light filtered in through a couple of small, frosted windows near the ceiling. I had not been back here in years and I wondered now at Jakob's and my courage to explore this haunting labyrinth of cells when we had been so young. But then, we had each other, and together we always felt invincible. Now, alone, I was frightened.

When I entered the passageway that connected the two buildings, all the light disappeared. I felt my way forward as quickly as caution would allow, knowing that if I stumbled and got injured, lives would be at stake. Thankfully the passage was not long and after a minute I saw dim light ahead. Relieved, I stepped into the cellar of my own building. This was more familiar territory as our family, together with several others in the building, stored our meagre supply of coal for the winter down here. I went to the less used back stairway and taking two steps at a time went up to the second floor where the Vargas lived, right across the courtyard from our own apartment. I prayed that Mother wouldn't look out our window at this moment. Would she be able to recognize me even though I was wearing these strange clothes?

My heart pounded in my chest as I knocked on the Vargas' door. Would they even be home? I hadn't really considered the possibility of their absence. I knew that Hendrik's father liked to catch up on his reading on Saturday afternoons and often his mother would use that opportunity to bake some tasty treats for the coming week. I hoped that today they were sticking to their regular routine. I tapped my foot impatiently.

At last the door opened and Magda, their maid stood there. A sweet, warm aroma followed her. For a second, she looked at me, confused. Then her face brightened.

"Why Ivan," she said, "I'm surprised to see you here. Hendrik said you would be off, busy with your father today. Hendrik is not here I'm afraid. He left first thing this morning on his bicycle saying he had to find some information at a bookstore for some sort of school assignment. Maybe you know which store he went to?"

"No, I don't. I'm not here for Hendrik. Please, I need to speak with Mr. and Mrs. Varga. It's urgent."

"Well certainly," she said. She opened the door wide. "I hope everything is alright. Come on in. Mr. Varga is just there in his study. I will fetch Mrs. Varga from the kitchen." She shut the door behind me and hurried off. Coming into the

Varga's home was pretty much like coming home. Because Hendrik/Jakob and I spent so much time together, we had become completely comfortable with each other's families over the years. Magda especially was like a second mother to both of us. Jakob had told me that she had been with their family since before he was born, helping in his mother's home before she married Mr. Varga. Magda always listened with great interest as we recounted our various adventures and often tended to the scrapes and bruises we acquired along the way.

I knocked on Mr. Varga's study door and went in without waiting for a reply.

"Why hello Ivan," he said as surprised as Magda had been, "what can I do for you? Where is Hendrik?" Everyone always assumed that when they saw one of us, the other would not be far behind. I swallowed, not really knowing how to answer that question. Before I could say anything, Mrs. Varga came into the room, wiping her hand on her apron.

"Hello, Ivan," she said, her voice sounding concerned "Magda mentioned that you wanted to speak to us. That it was urgent. Is it about Hendrik?

Is he alright?" Again, I swallowed and bit my lips together. Then, keenly aware of the passing of each minute, I blurted everything out.

"I know who you are," I started. "I mean, I know that you are Jewish." I caught the immediate look of alarm in Mr. Varga's eyes. Mrs. Varga let out a soft 'oh' and covered her mouth with her hand. She went to her husband's side and leaned into him. "I was in the ghetto in Pest today with Father," I hurried on. "It was horrible. Then all of a sudden, Hendrik was there, and he told Father that his real name was Jakob and that he was Jewish and Father got really angry and had him arrested and put on a truck. Then Father ordered me to come and alert the guards on the street about you, so that you could be arrested too. So I came, but I won't let them take you away. I – I haven't told the guards anything yet. You must leave at once! You must come with me!" I let out a big breath as I finished. Mrs. Varga collapsed onto her knees sobbing. Mr. Varga rose, took a step towards me and grabbed the front of my jacket in his fist.

"What are you saying?" he demanded, yanking me close to him. "Where is Hendrik? What was he doing in the ghetto? He had no business there. You are lying."

Chapter 11

"I'm not lying. I – I don't know what Hendrik was doing there – in the ghetto," I stammered. "But please, you have to hurry. You must believe me! You have to leave! Now!" Mr. Varga let go of me with such force that I almost fell. He turned and ran his fingers through his hair. I noticed for the first time that it was starting to turn gray at the sides.

"And where do you propose we go?" he asked with a snarl? "Aren't you the son of the Arrow Cross 'chief'? What are you doing here? Why aren't you at your father's side like you were supposed to be today? Or is this one of their tactics to lead us peacefully to the slaughterhouse? What I need to do now is find Hendrik. I need to make sure he is alright."

"No, No! You don't understand!" Unbidden tears spilled from my eyes. "I want to help. Hendrik, I mean Jakob, is my friend. But, but, I don't think there is anything you can do for him right now. The important thing at the moment is for you to get away. I will talk with Father about Hendrik after you are safe and once Father has calmed down. I promise! I will try to get Jakob back. Please come with me," I pleaded. "I know of a back route, a tunnel that will get us from here over to the next building. From there you can go to the Franciscan monastery. Brother Ferenc said he will hide you there till he can figure out what to do. You have to come before the guards in the street get here! Father might change his mind and send some of his men after all." I looked frantically from Mr. to Mrs. Varga.

"Why should I listen to you? A child!" Mr. Varga said. "You don't know what you are talking about. We are Catholics. I have papers to prove it. Tell me where Hendrik is being taken to."

"No. You don't understand," I said yet again. "I don't know where they are taking Hendrik but I will try to find out. Father believed that Hendrik was telling the truth. That his name is Jakob Kohn. Father told me to come back and tell the guards on our street to arrest you. But I came to warn you first. You have to leave now!" I was getting frustrated. I hadn't anticipated any opposition from them. Why couldn't he see that I was trying to help?

"Please Janos," Mrs. Varga said, her voice barely above a whisper, "I think we should listen to Ivan. Maybe he's right. Maybe Jakob overheard me talking with Magda the other day about my sister Mimi and how she was forced to move into the ghetto with Lilly and Gabor. Maybe that's why he went there. He used to be so fond of them."

"Yes," I said, looking at Mrs. Varga gratefully. "There was a woman with Jakob and a girl about our age." I did not mention the boy or rather the young man that had come running around the corner right after Father discovered Jakob; how he had called the woman that stood behind Jakob his mother. I dared not mention that he had resisted the guards and was immediately shot. There would be time later to talk about all that had happened in the ghetto and why. Right now, we needed to leave.

I saw a long, searching look pass between Mr. and Mrs. Varga. I saw Mr. Varga nod and his shoulders slump in resignation. I let out a sigh of relief.

"Very well," he said, "what do you propose we do?"

"We have to leave at once!" I repeated again. "I will show you the way to the passage through the other building. Right now!" I added in as commanding a voice as possible.

Mrs Varga stood up. "I have to pack. I need to get our valuables." She turned frantically from side to side, her eyes searching the corners of the room.

"No!" I shook my head. "There's no time. We must leave at once. Maybe I can come back later and collect some things you want, but there is no time now."

"If we're going to go, we'd best do as he says and leave immediately," Mr. Varga said.

"Very well, "Mrs. Varga said, "but Magda is coming with us too. I'm not leaving her behind. They will most likely take her away and question her then imprison her. It's forbidden for Christians to work for Jewish families now."

"Yes," I agreed, "Father said something about making sure that the guards arrest her too." Magda, who had followed Mrs. Varga into the room, looked at her with frightened eyes. Mrs. Varga stepped closer and wrapped her arms around their maid.

"Don't worry Magda," she said, "I will do everything in my power to make sure you are safe."

"Let's go then!" I said and walked towards the door hoping they would follow immediately. I used to imagine that giving out orders, especially to adults would give me a sense of importance and power, but this felt all wrong. I did not like having to tell the Vargas what they had to do. Ordering them around. But I did not have the luxury of time to worry about my feelings or theirs. This whole encounter had taken much too long. I needed to get back out on the street in my uniform and tell the guards to come and get the Vargas. We needed to go, now!

"We will follow you in a minute," Mr. Varga said, "We should appear as though we are going on a casual stroll. People are more likely to notice if we leave with you. The three of us have often gone out together in the past and since we live close to the back stairs, it's not unusual for us to take that route." I nodded and left, glad that he too was taking charge, attending to details that I failed to consider.

While I waited for them in the cellar, I quickly changed back into my Arrow Cross uniform. I was just retying my boots when they arrived. Mrs. Varga gasped when she saw me and clasped her hand over her mouth.

"My goodness Ivan," she said as I straightened up, "I didn't realize it was you. For an instant I thought that you had indeed led us into a trap."

"I'm sorry," I said, "I should have told you. Father borrowed this uniform for me for today, and I need to wear it when I tell the guards in the street to go to your apartment."

"You look like a grown man in that uniform," Mrs. Varga said. Despite her words, which I had such a short while ago longed to hear, I was unable to meet her eyes while dressed as an Arrow Cross soldier. I turned and led them through the dark tunnel into the cellar of the other building.

"I will come and see you as soon as I get a chance," I told them as we parted near the exit from the building's back stairway. "You must go straight to the Franciscan Monastery and ask for Brother Ferenc. He is expecting you. I will try to find out about Jakob and see if I can get him freed," I promised.

"And my sister Mimi, and her children," Mrs. Varga added in a pleading tone. "Please try to help them too!" She grasped my hands in both of hers and I nodded, knowing I was making a promise that I would probably not be able to keep.

"Thank you," she whispered and gave me a quick hug before stepping out into the sunlit courtyard and heading towards the front doors. Mr. Varga and Magda followed behind her.

Chapter 12

I waited as long as I dared to delay going to the guards in order to give the Vargas a good head start in getting to the monastery. Then I too stepped out, left the building and circled back around to my street. Immediately I saw Sergeant Balint who usually patrolled our street on Saturdays. He was talking with another Arrow Cross guard whom I didn't recognize. A Nazi soldier was standing a short way off, smoking a cigarette and observing them.

"Sergeant," I yelled as I ran up to him, trying to sound more out of breath than I actually was. "I have a message from Father. You must go and arrest the Vargas. It turns out they are Jews. They've been deceiving us. Father wants them rounded up immediately." I bent at the waist and clasped my knees as if trying to slow my breathing down. I did not want to look Sergeant Balint in the eye. I was scared that I might reveal some hint of my duplicity.

"The Vargas?" Sergeant Balint was taken aback. "Are you sure?" he asked, "your friend Hendrik's family? Aren't they Catholics? Doesn't Hendrik go to school with you at the Franciscan Friar's school?"

"Yes," I nodded, still keeping my head down, "but I guess it was all a guise. Father found Hendrik in the ghetto and Hendrik told him that his real name is Jakob Kohn and that he's Jewish."

Sergeant Balint let out a low whistle. "Well, that is a surprise!" he exclaimed. "But why would Hendrik do that?" he asked, "I mean if they were trying to hide their identity as Jews? Why would he suddenly tell your father?"

"I don't know," I said, slowly straightening up, "but Father is very angry at having been deceived. And so am I!" I hoped that I sounded sufficiently indignant. "We both want them punished. Father said they need to be captured before they suspect anything is wrong and try to leave. One of his soldiers drove me back partway, but we were stopped by a Nazi army convoy going up to the Citadel, so I ran the rest of the way to tell you."

"Well, you're a brave lad, not letting your friendship stand in the way of your duty," Sergeant Balint said and slapped me fondly on the shoulder. "I'm sure you'll be rewarded for your actions today. Maybe you'll be patrolling these streets with me sooner than you think." He too winked at me. He hollered to some of his men to come and follow him then turned towards our apartment building.

I let out a sigh of relief when he left and silently prayed that everything would work out as planned. I was glad that the sergeant had not asked me to accompany him. I had heard from Father how the soldiers often destroyed furniture and stole valuables from the Jewish homes they raided. I did not want to witness the destruction of the Vargas' home or be compelled to participate. If I refused, I'd have aroused suspicion.

I lingered in the area, waiting for the sergeant's return. I wanted to hear what his reaction would be after having failed to find the Vargas at home. I wondered what was happening with Jakob, with his aunt and cousin. I thought of the young man who died and shuddered at the memory of all that I had seen today. It was hard to admit to myself that just hours ago I had wanted to believe that the Arrow

Cross and the Nazis were right in their treatment of the Jews. That I wanted to carry a gun and fight in the war on their side. Again, I longed for the healing comfort of confession.

I thought back to Jakob's arguments. I had always responded by mimicking Father's words. Hid behind Father's authority. What if I had listened to Jakob more? Listened to his questions about the treatment of the Jews? What if I had revealed my own doubts and feelings to him? Could everything that had happened today have been avoided?

My thoughts were interrupted by the pounding of boots on the pavement as Sergeant Balint ran towards me followed by a couple of other Arrow Cross soldiers.

"They weren't home," he said with great urgency, "none of them. Not even their housekeeper. We knocked on some neighbours doors, even yours, but no one saw them go. No one had any idea where they may have gone. Judging by the dishes and half prepared food in the kitchen, they must have left in a hurry. There was even a pot of potatoes still simmering on the stove. Could they have suspected we were coming for them?"

"I don't think so," I said, shaking my head and drawing my brows together in puzzlement. "How could they have?" I pretended to be lost in thought for a moment. "Maybe they went to the theatre," I suggested, "or maybe just for a walk in the park. Hendrik has said that they like to do one or the other on Saturday afternoons. And they often take Magda, their housekeeper with them. She's like part of the family."

"Yes, those are good possibilities," Sergeant Balint nodded. "Tamas," he called to one of the other guards, "you and Robert go to the cinema on Feher Street and wait by the front entrance till the show is over. Arrest the Vargas and their housekeeper as soon as they come out if you see them. I will keep guard at the entrance to their building and will do the same if they return there from their walk." Turning back to me, Sergeant Balint once again slapped me lightly on the shoulder. "That was good thinking," he praised me. I silently agreed. Both the cinema and the park were several blocks in the opposite direction of the monastery. Hopefully the Vargas were safely hidden there by now.

I followed Sergeant Balint back to my building. There wasn't much left for me to do but go home and wait. Much as I wanted to, I dared not go back to see Brother Ferenc. That might jeopardize everything. At least, since our apartment was directly across the courtyard from the Varga's apartment. I would be able to keep an eye on their place and note any activity that took place there.

Chapter 13

Mother was surprised to see me back home so early, especially without Father. She was shocked when I told her of how we had discovered Hendrik in the ghetto. I made sure that with her I used the name Hendrik and not Jakob as I was now determined to call him both in my mind and with those whom I could trust with his true name.

"How dare the Vargas treat us like that?" Mother said with great indignation. "You must be very upset to have been so fooled by your best friend!" She wrapped her arms around me and pulled me close. For a moment I allowed myself to be comforted by her warmth.

I wished that I could unburden myself to Mother as I often had in the past. But I knew she would never dream of hiding anything about what I had just done from Father. She would never oppose him in any way. And I knew that she felt as Father did about the Jews. I couldn't risk her even suspecting the role that I had played in the Vargas' disappearance. Her concern for me now was for all the wrong reasons, but I could take advantage of that.

"Yes, I am upset," I said, pulling away from her. "I can't believe that Hendrik managed to hide that he's a Jew from me. I was his best friend!" I hoped that my anxiety over the Vargas fate would come across as anger in my voice. I picked my words carefully, not wanting to lie to Mother. Everything I said was true, I told myself – it was only the reasons behind my words that were different from what she believed.

"Well it wasn't totally Hendrik's fault," she said. "He is just a boy. He was probably only doing what his parents made him do. It's them that need to be punished."

Again, Brother Ferenc's words encouraging us to start taking responsibility for our actions came to mind, and with them, the growing suspicion that it was those same words that had motivated Jakob to go to the ghetto. The thought made me feel closer to Jakob. We had both been driven by the same intention.

"I'm going to my room. I need to think about everything that's happened," I said to Mother. She nodded; her eyes full of concern for me. I felt bad about deceiving her, but what else could I do?

I shut my bedroom door behind me, leaned against it and for the first time allowed myself to dwell on the enormity of everything that had taken place that day and the sudden choice that I had made. Tears sprang to my eyes as I thought of what Jakob and the Vargas must be going through at that moment. I thought of how dramatically their lives and mine had changed within the matter of a couple of hours. I thought of the promise I had made to the Vargas about trying to get Jakob back, knowing that I couldn't reveal to Father how I really felt and beg for his intervention on Jakob's behalf – not without endangering the lives of the entire family. I feared Father's reaction when he learned that Jakob's parents and their maid had disappeared. I feared what Father would do to me if he ever found out that I had helped them.

My room was on the right side of the front door of the apartment, the kitchen was on the left. Like the kitchen window, my bedroom window looked out into the courtyard. My desk and chair faced the window. The Varga's apartment had the same layout as ours and Jakob's bedroom window was directly across the courtyard from mine, his furniture set up the same way. Over the years, we had sat at our desks for countless hours sending secret messages in various formats across the expanse of the courtyard. If only I could send a message to him now, assuring him that his parents were safe and that I intended somehow to get him back to safety too.

I sat down at my desk and stared out. Across the way I could see an Arrow Cross soldier leaning his elbows on the railing in front of the Vargas' apartment, smoking a cigarette. I wondered how long their door would be guarded. Probably all night and even the next day. Father didn't give up easily, especially when he was angry.

I thought of the hours and days ahead of me at home with Father and Mother. Would I be able to keep pretending I didn't know where the Vargas were? That I had nothing to do with their disappearance? I had to if I wanted to protect them. And I would also have to pretend that I was as angry as Father about Jakob having deceived me, that I wanted to get back at him and punish him. That's what Father would expect.

I thought again of how much simpler life would be if I followed Father's orders. If I accepted what the Arrow Cross and Nazis were doing. But I knew with a certainty that I had not felt before that I could not do that. I had seen too much of the suffering inflicted on the Jews. And more importantly, I knew in my heart that they were people that deserved respect, just like everyone else.

I buried my face in my hands. I re-lived the horror of the moment when the shot rang out and the young man's body crumpled to the ground. Of how I had stood there, unable to do anything. Unable to help anybody. I recalled the look in Jakob's eyes when he noticed me. Did he understand that I couldn't do anything right then and there to help even though I wanted to? That I couldn't openly challenge Father in front of his men (or ever, without grave consequences)? Or did he think that I was on Father's side, agreeing with whatever he said? Did he think that I was no longer his friend?

I sat, brooding over these thoughts by the window as the late afternoon shadows lengthened and the courtyard became obscured in the early evening gloom. The soldier across the way was replaced by another. I heard Mother's supper preparations in the kitchen. She had come to my door once, knocking gently and asked if there was anything I wanted, anything that she could do for me. I told her that I was fine, that I just wanted to be alone for now. She had hesitated before her soft steps retreated down the hallway, back to the kitchen.

Mother was generally cheerful and kind. She was friends with most of our neighbours, helping them out whenever someone was ill or upset over something. When Father was angry and worried, she knew what words would soothe his temper, what foods would calm him down and restore his composure. The few wrinkles she occasionally complained about only helped to accentuate her smiling face. I marveled now how someone like her could also, at the same time, support the Arrow Cross and their treatment of the Jews. How could she be so proud of Father and all that he was doing?

It was dark and the aromas drifting in from the kitchen were making my stomach growl before I heard Father's heavy footsteps come along the balcony that circled each floor of the courtyard. The moment had come. I took a deep breath, said a quick, silent prayer and hurried out of my room to meet him.

"Father!" I rushed up to him, without waiting for a greeting, "Do you have any news about the Vargas? Have they been captured?" Seeing Father's frowning face, I worried for a moment that I was perhaps too eager and would arouse his suspicions, but despite his drawn brows, Father smiled at me and shook his head.

"No, I'm afraid not," he said, "no one has seen them. But both my chauffeur and Sergeant Balint told me what an excellent job you did in assisting with the hunt. How you ran back here on foot when you encountered a traffic blockage and suggested places where the Vargas might be found. I'm proud of you, Ivan!" He gripped both my shoulders in his powerful hands as he looked me in the eye. "I was worried for a while there in the ghetto, but you have conducted yourself well today! I hope that soon I can give you more opportunities to prove yourself."

It was easy to smile back at Father on hearing that no trace of the Vargas had been found, though I knew that he would assume that my smile was a response to his praise. Mother came over to us from the kitchen.

"It is distressing to discover that Jews had been living here, right under our nose, all these years," she said as she reached up to rub Father's arm. "Ivan has told me what happened. But come, you have both had a long, tiring day. I have some hot chicken soup with dumplings all ready. Come and eat and you can tell us all that has happened in detail over supper."

Chapter 14

"Where did Hendrik get taken?" was the first thing I asked after swallowing a large mouthful of the delicious soup. "When will he be coming back?"

"Humph," Father snorted, "I don't think you'll be seeing your deceitful ex- friend any time soon," he said. "Hopefully never again."

"Why? What is going to happen to him?" I hoped that I sounded angry instead of concerned.

"He was taken to the Western Train Station along with all the other vermin that were rounded up today. They will be put on trains and taken to a labour camp. Auschwitz, I believe is where the Nazis are transporting them these days. It's in Poland. Though of course, like many other European countries these days, Poland is under German rule."

"A labour camp?" I said, still trying to keep an edge of anger to my voice. "That doesn't sound that bad. Hendrik and I both got used to hard physical work over the summer. He might actually enjoy it."

"Don't be too sure of that," Father laughed. "Auschwitz is not your regular labour camp. People go there to die. Many are exterminated right away. Those that are too old or too weak or too young to be of use. The others are put to work until they too die from the starvation diet or disease. Once they aren't any further use as labourers." He picked up a chicken leg between two fingers and missed the shock that I knew must have shown on my face. I couldn't let Jakob go there. Nor that young girl, who I now figured must be his cousin, who had stood behind him. She had already looked too weak and pale. She would never survive the harsh conditions Father had just described. I had to do something to stop them from getting to Auschwitz.

"What if he escapes somehow?" I asked. "He's good at sneaking around. At going unnoticed."

"The train that Hendrik would be travelling on isn't your regular train either," Father said with satisfaction. "Maybe that's where I'll take you next time, to the train station so you can see for yourself. No," Father shook his head, "the train that Hendrik would be on isn't a comfortable passenger train. It's a freight train – a string of cattle cars – suitable for animals such as the ones he's travelling with. That's how we transport Jews and other prisoners like the gypsies and those people foolish enough to try to help them. We squeeze well over a hundred people on to one of the cars, though the weakling SS officially recommended only fifty."

We ate in silence for a moment. Neither Father nor Mother were aware of the turmoil Father's words had caused in my heart and mind. Until this moment I had been ignorant of what happened to the people that had been rounded up by the Nazis and the Arrow Cross.

"I must admit," Father continued, "that I'm thankful that I have never been asked to accompany one of those trains to their destination. I've heard stories of the unbearable stench that billows out every time the doors are opened. The trip generally lasts several days and the only thing those people have to relieve themselves in is one small bucket per car. Though they are emptied at every stop, the buckets are more than overflowing by then. Plus, apparently about a third of the people don't even survive the train ride; so, added to the stench of the buckets is that of decaying bodies as well." Even Father seemed disgusted at that thought.

"Well, what bothers me," Mother spoke up, probably trying to divert the conversation somewhat from this unappetizing angle, "is that those people lived right here in the building with us. With us!" she emphasized. "And I spoke with Rose Varga almost every day. We exchanged recipes. I had coffee with her. I even hugged her. I thought she was a friend. Can you imagine?" She shook her head. "It makes me suspicious of everyone I know." Again, I wondered how Mother who was so good to us, could be so insensitive to the plight of the Jews.

I hung my head as if in sympathy with Mother's shame and disgust, but what I needed was time to think. I had to do something to get Jakob and his aunt and cousin off that train before it was too late.

"Of course, I could have had Hendrik shot on the spot and order the same for his parents and housekeeper as soon as they're found," Father said, "but then they would have been denied the pleasure of that train ride and the joys of life at Auschwitz. Don't worry dear," Father reached over and squeezed Mother's hand, "they will pay royally for what they have done to us."

"What if you have Hendrik brought back here, and let *me* deal with him?" I asked suddenly as it occurred to me that that would at least save Jakob from the camp and buy me some time. I could pretend to punish Jakob without actually hurting him. And then we could pretend that he somehow escaped. If only I could get him off that train first, I would figure out the rest after. I wished that I could help the others as well, but Jakob was my main concern.

"No. That's not possible," Father said. "The trains are guarded by the SS. They wouldn't want me interfering with their authority. Besides," Father added with a look of satisfaction, "though I appreciate your wish for revenge, I don't think anything you can do to Hendrik could equal the suffering he is in for at the hands of the Nazis."

"Do you think that the Vargas will be found?" I asked Father. He thought for a long moment.

"I don't know," he admitted at last, rubbing his forehead. "Unfortunately there are people working against us. People willing to risk their lives to hide and protect these undesirable vermin. People who should be imprisoned as well! The problem is that often we don't know who they are. Or they have too many safeguards around them." Father's tone was becoming angry.

"Like that hateful man, Wallenberg. We suspect, no, we know that he is giving out false Swedish identity papers that the Nazis honor! They never question their legitimacy. Just because it looks official on paper." Father's voice rose as his anger increased. "But not us. Not the Arrow Cross!" Father slammed his fist down on the table making the bowls bounce and splash soup over their sides. "We are not fools!" he was almost shouting now, "We will rid Hungary of all this pestilence!"

"Tomas," Mother said gently and laid a comforting hand on Father's arm. "I have all the confidence that with your direction, we will succeed."

"Yes Father," I agreed. "And I will do everything I can to help you," For the first time that I could remember, I deliberately lied to Father.

Chapter 15

Monday, Nov. 7

I had never looked forward to school as eagerly as I did that Monday morning. I would finally get to see Brother Ferenc and get assurance from him that the Vargas were safe. Also, I hoped to get his advice about how I might get Jakob and his aunt and cousin back.

The day before, on Sunday, though it was his day off, Father insisted on helping in the search for the Vargas.

"I don't understand how they just disappeared," he grumbled again at supper time. "No one seems to have seen them walk out the front door of this building. Not even the guards posted at each corner. You're sure you didn't see them leaving their apartment at any time?" He asked Mother yet again.

"Honestly, Tomas," Mother sounded exasperated. "I've told you over and over, I don't have time to just sit by the window and watch everyone's comings and goings. Not like old Irma Nagy. That's all she does all day, except for when she naps in the afternoon, that is."

"And with my luck, that's precisely when the Vargas slipped away. I just don't understand how they knew to disappear right when their son so conveniently fell into my arms. Well," he added with satisfaction, "at least we have him. When Hendrik doesn't return to them, I'm sure the Vargas will take some blundering step in their attempt to find him and thereby reveal their whereabouts. I will not stop until I've hunted them down."

Father's words increased my anxiety for the Vargas' wellbeing, but there was nothing I could do until Monday - no words of caution I could send to the monastery. I didn't dare arouse Father's suspicion by going there on a Sunday, which I had never done before.

I missed Jakob's presence throughout that long day of waiting. Though we were Catholic and I attended the Franciscan's school for boys with

Jakob, my family did not go to church regularly and until now, we had assumed that Jakob's family was like us, not really taking their religion all that seriously. Jakob and I usually spent Sundays together. We explored various parts of the city on our bikes, invented all sorts of games and adventures or went to the local park to kick around a soccer ball with other guys in the neighbourhood. But this Sunday I moped around aimlessly, worrying about what was happening to Jakob. I tried to imagine what it was like for him wedged in among a hundred other frightened people in a cattle car. What must he be thinking and feeling?

At last, Monday morning arrived, and I hurried off to school. It felt strange to be walking by myself. My first class was math followed by literature, both taught by Franciscan friars other than Brother Ferenc. It wasn't until the period just before lunch that I had religion class with Brother Ferenc in which he began to explain the meaning of the first statement of the Catholic Creed.

"Every Sunday, during Mass, we recite the Creed," he said towards the end of the class. "If you are not in the habit of attending Sunday Mass, I would recommend that you start doing so. You are old enough now that you no longer need to rely on your parents to bring you here to the church. I know that many of your parents prefer to relax at home on Sundays, but you can take the initiative and come on your own. Especially those of you who live nearby."

I wished that he had given this advice last week. If I could have used his recommendation as the excuse to go to church yesterday, I would have been able to get news of the Vargas then. Throughout the class Brother Ferenc hadn't given any hint that a special connection now existed between us. However, as we gathered our books and headed towards the dining hall, he called out to me.

"Ivan, can you stay behind for a moment please. I would like to have a word with you." It wasn't unusual for Brother Ferenc to want to discuss something or other with one of the boys. Nobody payed much attention to his request, but my heart began to race with anticipation as I made my way towards his desk. We waited till the last boy left the room and pulled the door closed behind him. Brother Ferenc pulled up a chair and motioned for me to sit.

"The Vargas and their housekeeper arrived safely without any complications," he began, and I let out a long sigh of relief. At least they were fine for the time being. "You did well in thinking of bringing them to me. I know it must have been difficult for you to go against your father's wishes. I have hidden them in one of the empty guest rooms in the East wing," Brother Ferenc continued. "It's where men stay when they come here for retreats or for more intense formation. Unfortunately, the Vargas and their housekeeper cannot stay there much longer." He bowed his head for a moment and sighed.

"I must admit that we are a house divided on this issue of the Jews. I'm not sure which of my brothers, if any, I can trust completely. None of us approve of the harshness with which the Nazis and the Arrow Cross treat people in general, but regarding the Jews," Brother Ferenc grimaced and shook his head. "Many of my brothers openly admit that they think their treatment is justified. But," he smiled, "I managed to get the Vargas to the room without anyone noticing. Fortunately, they arrived when all the brothers were in the library at study. Except for me of course," he added and winked at me. "Thanks to you, I was on the lookout for them and stayed by the door. They didn't even have to ring the bell."

'A house divided'. So, the Vargas weren't safe, not even here.

Chapter 16

"What can we do? Where can they stay if not here?" I asked. Brother Ferenc held up a hand to calm my obvious anxiety.

"I have been thinking," he said, tapping his forehead with a finger. "The Papal Nuncio, Monsignor Rotta, is the Pope's representative here in Hungary. I know that he sympathizes with the unjust plight of the Jews and is secretly trying to help. He is in collaboration with a man, Raul Wallenberg, a Swedish diplomat who has been forging documents giving Swedish protection to Jews, claiming that they are Swedish citizens. The Nazis respect those documents and will honor them. They will not deport anyone who has one."

"But that's great!" I said, remembering Father's anger towards Wallenberg. "That means everyone, I mean all the Jews, can get a document and be saved." Brother Ferenc smiled sadly and shook his head.

"I wish it were that simple," he said. "Each document needs to have the person's name and a photograph on it as well as other particulars. Mr. Wallenberg can't get photographs of everyone, especially once they've been arrested. Those photographs can only be obtained from documents like passports that have been left behind. And it all has to be done secretly. Mr. Wallenberg, Monsignor Rotta and others who are also trying to help can't save everyone, but they are doing the best they can."

"Mr. Wallenberg has also set up some 'safe houses' which are designated as Swedish property and therefore also under Swedish protection," Brother Ferenc continued. "For now at least, the Nazis do not go into these buildings. So Jews, even without the necessary forged papers can be hidden there. I have contacted Monsignor Rotta and begged his help for the Vargas and their housekeeper. He has promised to get in touch with Mr. Wallenberg immediately and find room for the Vargas in one of the safe houses. I hope we can move them out of here before curfew this evening."

Again, I let out a sigh of relief. And again, Brother Ferenc held up a cautionary hand.

"Unfortunately, the Arrow Cross are not as respectful of the protection offered by the Swedish. They grumble about this 'leniency' of the Nazis and are itching to defy them. It is imperative that your father does not suspect that the Vargas are in one of these buildings."

"I know," I said, feeling ashamed on behalf of my father. "Father complains about the weakness of the Nazis a lot." It was a strange experience, feeling shame on account of Father instead of pride. But I had no time to dwell on that.

"What about Jakob?" I asked. "Can we get him back? And his aunt and cousin? Father said that Jakob is on a train. A horrible train taking hundreds of Jews to a place called Auschwitz. Father said it's a place where people are forced to work really hard and are starving. And many are killed. We can't let Jakob get there. Is there anything we can do to get him back?" My voice broke on the last couple of words. It seemed so hopeless. I felt a tear trickle down my cheek, but I was beyond caring about the kind of impression I made. There were far more important things at stake here.

Brother Ferenc was lost in thought for a few moments before replying. "It's been done before," he said at last. "I heard that Wallenberg has gotten people right off the trains with his passes. I will make enquiries immediately. If the train hasn't crossed the border yet, it might be possible. But as I said, we will need photographs, both of Jakob and his relatives."

"I will get them." I said with more confidence than I felt. Brother Ferenc didn't question how I was going to manage that.

"Good," he said. "We'll need them as soon as possible. Now, you'd best get to the dining room and have some lunch while there is some food left for you." I got up and went to the door.

"Do you think that I can see Mr. and Mrs. Varga sometime?" I asked turning back to Brother Ferenc. "I want to let them know how sorry I am about everything that's happened. And I now have so many questions now about them and Jakob and how they managed to pretend to be Catholic all this time."

"Let's get them settled in a safe house first," said Brother Ferenc. "And let's try to get Jakob and his aunt and cousin back. Then hopefully, once everyone is together and safe, there will be plenty of time to talk. I will let the Vargas know that you are doing everything in your power to help them."

Chapter 17

I couldn't pay much attention during my afternoon classes. I was too busy plotting out how to get the necessary photographs for Brother Ferenc to pass on to Mr. Wallenberg. It all had to happen today if there was any hope of getting Jakob and his relatives off the train before it crossed the Hungarian border. Who knows, maybe it was already too late, but we had to try everything possible.

By the time school let out at 2:30pm, I had a plan. I raced all the way home.

"Mother," I called as soon as I burst through our front door, "I have to try to get into the Vargas apartment. Brother Ferenc needs me to return a book that he had lent Hendrik last week. I need to go over and find it. Hopefully that guard will let me in." I had noticed that there was still a guard positioned on the balcony across the courtyard. He was slouched in a chair beside the Vargas' door. And it was true that Jakob had borrowed a book from Brother Ferenc last week that he had promised to return today.

"But what about the Levente?" she asked, sounding worried. "You're supposed to go there every day after school! You'll get into trouble if you don't go." She was right. Military training with the Levente organization was compulsory for all boys over twelve years old. Every day, as soon as school let out, Jakob and I had hurried over to the local training centre where attendance was always taken.

"Everyone misses training occasionally," I said lightly, as if it didn't matter much. But I knew that the next day I would be required to do at least a dozen extra push-ups, with my entire troop watching. It was humiliating to be singled out like that, but for once I didn't care.

"Well, in that case, I'll come with you to the Vargas' apartment," Mother offered. "Maybe I will see a few things that I could keep. I always admired Rose's lace tablecloth. I should get it before the Nazis loot the place."

"No, Mother," I said quickly. I couldn't let her come with me and see what I was really there to get. I looked down at my shoes as if embarrassed to admit my feelings. "Please, I would rather do this on my own. It will be difficult to go in there knowing who Hendrik really is. This first time I would like to be alone."

"Very well," she said, patting my shoulder. "I guess I can go on my own later. Perhaps with your father when he gets home." I didn't wait to hear more. I turned and left.

As I walked around the balcony and neared the guard, he pulled himself upright on the chair, then stood at attention. I saluted him.

"I'm Sergeant Biro's son," I said and pointed to my door. "I live just across the way there. The boy who lived here went to my school and he had borrowed a book from my teacher. I need to find it and return it. You don't need to come in with me," I added, just in case. "I know my way around the apartment and know which is Hendrik's room. You can go back to your rest." I tried to speak with the authority and confidence that I always saw Father display. The guard smiled at me.

"Go ahead in, the lock's been broken," he said, slumping back down on the chair. "You must be Ivan. I've heard about you. You're a brave lad."

"Thanks," I said. "I shouldn't be too long."

"Well, don't be surprised if the book isn't quite where you expect it to be," he said. "The place has been," there was a slight pause as he tried to find the right words, "well searched," he finally added with a chuckle.

I stepped inside, suddenly fearing that the photographs I had come to find would be gone or destroyed. But though the place was in disarray, with furniture and ornaments knocked over, it didn't look like the apartment had been looted yet. At least not that I could tell.

I easily found a picture of Jakob taken just this past summer. It was in a small gilded frame that I recalled had stood on the mahogany sideboard in the dining room. It now lay on the floor, the glass over Jakob's smiling face, cracked. With nervous fingers I removed the photograph from its frame and slipped it in my pocket. With equal ease I found photographs of Mr. and Mrs. Varga and even one of Magda – one in which she and Mrs. Varga stood side by side with their arms around each other's waist. Though these weren't as important to have, I pocketed them as well, just in case.

I couldn't see any photographs of Jakob's aunt and cousin and didn't recall ever seeing any on display. They were part of the family though. Even if a secret part. Wouldn't Mrs. Varga have a picture of them somewhere? Hidden away? I went into the Vargas' bedroom and started pulling out dresser drawers and rummaged through their contents. Nothing.

I could come back, I told myself, with some other excuse, after I had a chance to ask Mrs. Varga about any existing photographs. Except, by then it would probably be too late. Any delay meant that the chances of intercepting their train before it reached its destination, were greatly reduced.

I leaned my back against the wall and closed my eyes, trying to imagine where else Mrs. Varga may have hidden pictures of her sister and niece. I remembered once seeing Mother slip some bills between the clean sheets in our linen cabinet.

"Its money that I saved for Father's birthday gift," she had explained when she saw me notice.

"Men never think of looking for anything where the linens are kept."

I went back into the hallway and opened the doors of a large cabinet across from the bathroom door. It was filled with towels, sheets and lace tablecloths. I slid my hands between and behind every item. Finally, on the second shelf from the bottom, against the back wall, behind the sheets, my fingers encountered a thin box. I pulled it out, opened it and saw right away that indeed it contained several photographs. I readily found pictures of the woman and young girl I had seen in the ghetto as well as of the young man who had been shot and an older man, probably Mrs. Varga's brother in law. I slid the box with it's contents inside my jacket. Next, I easily found the book Jakob had borrowed on the floor beside his bed.

Within minutes I was back outside on the courtyard's balcony.

"I found it!" I said triumphantly, holding up the book to show the guard.

My mission had been successful.

Chapter 18

After telling Mother that I was returning to the school to give Brother Ferenc the book, I took off again.

"You are amazing!" Brother Ferenc slapped me good naturedly on the shoulder when, out of breath, I handed him both the book and my stash of photographs. Once again, I had come to the main monastery building and he led me to the same small office on one side of the main foyer.

"You know," he said with a sly smile, "you could be a real asset to the effort of rescuing Jews from the Nazis and Arrow Cross. No one suspects you. You're young and full of energy and your father is an Arrow Cross Sergeant. You're probably privy to all kinds of information that could be helpful." Then Brother Ferenc shook his head.

"No. What am I thinking? It's out of the question." He shook his head again and turned away. "It would be way too dangerous. If your father ever found out that you are actively working against him…" his voice trailed off. "I can't let you do that," he resumed. "Your father is a clever man. Sooner or later he would find out."

"Not if I'm careful!" I exclaimed. His words had sent a charge of energy through me. "Father doesn't suspect me at all regarding the Vargas." I reached out and grabbed Brother Ferenc's arm, surprised at how thin his biceps felt under his brown Franciscan habit. "I want to help! I need to." I insisted. "I can't just stand by and do nothing now that I know what is going on. I want to help more people, other than just the Vargas. And you're right. I could get valuable information from Father. He treats me like a man now. He trusts me." I couldn't help but let a bit of pride slip into that last statement.

"Well, we will see," Brother Ferenc said quietly. He looked at his watch. "In the meantime, I have heard from Monsignor Rotta. He told me that Mr. Wallenberg is sending a vehicle here in about an hour to pick up the Vargas. Again, it will be at a time when most of my brothers are at prayer so the chances of the Vargas being noticed are diminished. I will send these photographs with them and maybe by tomorrow the documents will be ready and the train can be stopped. Apparently, Hendrik – I mean Jakob, I too will start calling him that – is on a train that is meandering through some towns to the east to pick up more prisoners. It gives us more of an opportunity to intercept it before it leaves the country. There is still hope."

Yes, I nodded at his words, there was hope. I felt elated that I had been able to play a part in furnishing that hope. I wanted to do more of this! Brother Ferenc and Mr. Wallenberg had to let me to continue to help them. Maybe I would be able to speak with Mr. Wallenberg directly and persuade him.

"Where is the safe house that the Vargas are going to?" I asked.

"I believe they are being taken directly to the Swedish Legation building on Minerva Street. They have a room for them to stay in there. Because it's the Arrow Cross and, in particular, your father, who are looking for them, Mr. Wallenberg thought that would be the safest for now. As I mentioned earlier, the Arrow Cross are in many ways more ruthless than the German Nazis."

I hung my head, once again ashamed of my father and his role in all of this. How could he be like that? How could he not see the wrongness of what he was a part of? I wondered if I would ever be able to talk to him about it without revealing my role in saving the Varga family, without endangering their lives or others.

"It's not your fault how your father is behaving," Brother Ferenc said as if reading my thoughts. "Remember, Jesus asked God, his Father to forgive his executioners because they did not know what they were doing. If your father knew, if he truly understood the evil of what he is participating in, I believe that he would not only turn from it, but he would vigorously fight against it. As his son, your duty is to love him for whatever goodness there is in him, and as far as you are able, do what is right."

"It's difficult," I confessed, suddenly wavering in my enthusiasm to help Mr. Wallenberg's cause. "And confusing."

"I know," Brother Ferenc said, "but I'm confident that your heart will lead you in the right direction. And whenever you need advice, I will try to help you as best I can. Now, I'd best be on my way to see that the Vargas get away as planned and to pass these photographs on to Mr. Wallenberg and his men." I turned to go, knowing that I shouldn't detain Brother Ferenc any longer.

"I will let you know everything that happened when I see you in school tomorrow," Brother Ferenc promised as I shut the door behind me.

I looked at my watch. If I hurried, I would be only about an hour late for the Levente training. Maybe I would avoid the humiliation of the extra push-ups.

Chapter 19

Wednesday, Nov.8

By Wednesday morning, the boys in my class had started asking questions. Where's Hendrik? How come he's been absent for two days? Is he sick? Questions that I wasn't sure how to answer. I didn't know if telling them the truth would cause extra problems or not. I shrugged and said I didn't know.

Then in the dining room during our lunch break, Zoltan, the class bully, announced in a loud voice that he heard that Hendrik and his family were Jews and that they had been deported. A shocked murmur spread around the dining room.

"I bet you knew all along that your little friend was a Jew," Zoltan sneered as he turned towards me and pointed his finger at my face. "I bet you knew and you never said anything. Not even after all the Jews were ordered to wear a yellow star. You've been protecting him all along."

"I – I didn't know," I stammered, unprepared for the accusation. "Hendrik never told me anything." While I wasn't afraid of Zoltan, I had never openly disagreed with him. Jakob and I had generally avoided any interaction with him. We ignored all the petty ways in which he tormented the boys that were smaller than he. In build, Hendrik and I were at least his equal and until now, we had had the advantage of our friendship, so Zoltan had left us alone.

"Yeah right!" Zoltan challenged now. "Are you trying to tell me that you were best friends for years and he never told you his secret? Some kind of strange friendship that would be. And what does your famous Arrow Cross Sergeant father think of it all? I bet he's not so proud of his Jew loving son now. Maybe he'll get you deported as well along with the rest of them," he laughed. I felt my face turn crimson.

"It's not true!" I said, almost shouting. We were both standing now facing each other across the two rows of tables between us. "I didn't know anything about Hendrik being Jewish. My Father knows that. He's angry because they had deceived all of us. He had even asked me to help in rounding them up."

I hated what my words implied. That I was on the side of those who hated the Jews. That I too wanted them deported. But I had seen the cost of telling the truth in the ghetto. I would be of no help to anyone if I said the wrong thing, in the heat of the moment. I would not make Hendrik's mistake.

"Yeah, well I don't believe you. I'm not an idiot. My mom said that she heard at the butcher's that Hendrik's parents had disappeared by the time the guards got to their place. Maybe you had something to do with that? Maybe you didn't give exactly the kind of help your father had asked for."

Zoltan *was* an idiot. In the past he had accused others in the class of being guilty of all sorts of trivial misdemeanors, most of which he had perpetrated himself. But he had come dangerously close to the truth this time. I had to divert his suspicions.

In an instant I leaped over my table, reached across his and grabbed the front of Zoltan's shirt with my left hand. I pulled him towards me.

"Don't you dare call me a liar!" I hissed at him. "Don't you dare call me any names at all!" I was about to punch him with my right fist when a strong hand gripped my shoulder.

"That's enough Ivan," Brother Ferenc's deep voice boomed above me. I had not noticed him entering the dining room. "Come and see me in my office after school." All the anger and fear drained out of me. I was confident that Brother Ferenc would understand what was going on once I explained things to him. I was glad that he hadn't asked Zoltan to join us for his reprimand. I didn't mind taking all the blame for now. And because of that, I ignored Zoltan's triumphant grin as Brother Ferenc turned and walked away.

What concerned me more was the troubled look I detected in Brother Ferenc's eyes before he turned his back on us. Was he so dismayed at my behaviour? Or had something bad happened? Had the Vargas been discovered? Had they too been forced onto a train headed to Auschwitz? Or perhaps the rescue effort to get Jakob and his relatives off the train had been too late and they were beyond anyone's ability to help them.

These and other such thoughts distracted me from my lessons throughout the afternoon. At the end of the school day, I hurried to Brother Ferenc's office in the school building.

"Have a seat," he said, indicating a plain wooden chair, while he stood and paced back and forth in front of me. I sat down without a word, my heart pounding violently in my chest, fearing what he would say. It was my first time in here and I glanced around at the bare walls adorned only by a simple wooden crucifix facing Brother Ferenc's desk. The desk too was simple, old and worn. Everything in here matched the sparse décor of the school building and the adjoining monastery. I knew that the Franciscan brothers practiced a strict vow of poverty and while they apparently spared no expense in providing us with the best education possible, they themselves lived a very frugal life. The only items on Brother Ferenc's desk were an open book and a small, ceramic statue of the Virgin Mary.

"I don't know how to tell you this," Brother Ferenc finally stopped his pacing and stood in front of me. "But you will find out eventually." He took a deep breath and went on, while I listened with mounting apprehension. Clearly this was not about something as trivial as my run in with Zoltan in the dining room.

"Mr. Wallenberg and his assistant managed to reach the train transporting Jakob, his aunt and cousin," Brother Ferenc said quietly, almost as if he hoped I wouldn't hear. "They had all the necessary papers, all forged with the appropriate photographs attached, thanks to you." He smiled at me briefly, then continued. "They stopped the train just a few kilometers before it reached the border. They ordered the German Nazis to search for any of the Swedish Nationals for whom they had documentation. Wallenberg hoped to rescue more than just Jakob and his family. The guards went from car to car, opening the doors and calling out the names on the documents. Jakob's aunt, cousin and several others got off and the guards herded them over to Wallenberg's truck at gunpoint. All those poor people must have thought that they were about to be executed. Unfortunately, there seemed to be no sign of Jakob himself. Wallenberg insisted that they call for him again, which they did, but still without success."

"I'm sorry," Brother Ferenc said. He bent down to look me in the eye and gripped my shoulders, "I'm sorry to have to tell you that they came back without Jakob."

Chapter 20

I sat stunned, hoping that I had misunderstood Brother Ferenc.

"Without Jakob?" I asked. "But why? Why would they come back without Jakob? Couldn't they keep looking? Maybe Jakob was on a different train."

"No," Brother Ferenc shook his head sadly, "Jakob's name was on the Nazis' list for that train. They keep meticulous track of everything. And apparently Jakob's aunt saw him at one point when they were stopped and ordered to get off the cars briefly. But that had been on the previous day. When Wallenberg had the Nazis call Jakob's name he didn't respond. We don't know why, but we must be prepared for the worst. Many people don't survive the train ride. The conditions there are horrible I've heard. Often the dead aren't noticed until they arrive at the camps."

"That's ridiculous," I yelled. I shrugged off Brother Ferenc's hands and jumped up. "Jakob is strong and healthy. Not like many of the other people I saw rounded up in the ghetto. His cousin, she's the one that looked so weak as though she could barely stand. If she's still alive, then so is Jakob."

"Let's hope you are right," agreed Brother Ferenc. "Mrs. Varga certainly thinks the same way as you do – that there had to be some other reason why Jakob didn't respond. Why he didn't get off the train. I'm afraid we won't know the answer to that now until all this is over." He waved his hand in the air as if including all of time, all of the world.

I slumped back onto the chair and leaned forward, my elbows on my knees, my face in my hands. I refused to believe that Jakob was dead. Instead, I tried to imagine what must be happening to him right now. Was there anything else I could have done? Anything else that I could still do? What if I told Father? What if I told him what I had done and why? What if I tried to get him to see? To see that Jakob and his family were not bad just because they were Jewish, that they had deceived us only so that they could save their lives – lives that shouldn't have been in danger in the first place.

But when I thought of Father, of his pride, of his fiery anger, of how he hated to be challenged by anyone about anything, even if it was Mother or I, I realized there was no hope. Not through him. I would only make things much worse for the Vargas. I might get all of them killed. And then if Jakob was still alive, if one day he did come back, it would be for nothing, to no one, after all he had gone through. No, I decided. I would do whatever was in my power to protect his family without breathing a word to Father.

I looked up and saw Brother Ferenc quietly studying me with a concerned expression on his face.

"Would you like to come with me to the Swedish Legation?" he asked when our eyes met. "I think it might be good for both you and the Vargas to talk. Perhaps you will even meet Mr. Wallenberg."

"Yes," I said eagerly, jumping up. Going with Brother Ferenc would mean that this time I would most likely completely miss my Levente military training. I didn't care. The punishment was easily worth it. I needed to do something. Anything to take my mind off of all the bad things that were happening one after another. And maybe I would find some way to keep searching for Jakob. Or, as Brother Ferenc had hinted a couple of days ago, I could help Mr. Wallenberg in his efforts to rescue more Jews.

"Mother isn't expecting me home for quite a while yet because I usually go straight to the local Levente centre," I said. "It won't matter if I miss a day. Let's go!"

Chapter 21

I felt self-conscious walking down the street with a Franciscan friar especially at a time of day when most boys my age were expected to be at military training centres. Brother Ferenc had pulled on a long black overcoat on top of his brown cassock, but his brown habit protruded out the bottom and its hood covered his bald head. However, nobody seemed to pay much attention to us.

For the first time I noticed that most people walked with downcast eyes. No one wanted to be singled out or recognized by the patrolling Nazis and Arrow Cross. The slightest misstep or wrong word could lead to an endless interrogation and maybe land you in jail. To my relief, the guards ignored the two of us.

As the main streetcar track had been badly damaged in a recent attack by the Russian forces advancing on Hungary, we had to take a roundabout bus route to reach Minerva Street. The Swedish legation building was a large yellow, palatial edifice. It was surrounded by a fancy stone wall that was interrupted in places by wrought iron fencing that gave a glimpse of the narrow grounds circling the building. I was surprised to see a crowd of anxious looking men and women lined up outside in front of the main gate.

"They are all Jews, hoping to get the Swedish protection papers," Brother Ferenc whispered to me. He led me around the corner to a smaller gateway which was almost concealed from sight by the tangle of barren ivy stems covering much of the stone wall. He rattled the metal frame of the gate and a Swedish guard stepped out from behind the stone wall, nodded in recognition of Brother Ferenc, unlocked the gate and let us in.

We entered the building through a metal side door. I followed Brother Ferenc down a maze of polished granite hallways lined with closed doors and up a flight of stairs. I couldn't help thinking what fun it would be to explore this building with Jakob. I could imagine it having a number of secret rooms and passageways; many concealed nooks in which to hide. Finally, Brother Ferenc stopped at a door that stood open. Still, he knocked before entering.

"Ah, Brother Ferenc," a tall man, who had been standing behind a desk, hurried over to us. He shook Brother Ferenc's hand then looked at me and smiled. "Is this the young man who saved the life of your friends?" he asked, reaching out to shake my hand as well. I instinctively liked him. He looked to be somewhat younger than Father, though I was not good at guessing how old people were. Jakob was way better at that. Another man who was sitting behind the desk glanced up at me at his words.

"Yes," Brother Ferenc replied, patting me on the back, "this is our man, Ivan. Ivan, this is Mr. Wallenberg. He is responsible for rescuing Jakob's relatives."

"You did well, Ivan, in alerting Mr. and Mrs. Varga and their housekeeper to the danger they faced," Mr. Wallenberg said. "It was very courageous of you to do that behind your father's back. I wish we had more boys like you to help us out." I felt myself blush at his praise.

"I – I wish I could have done more," I stammered. "In the ghetto, I mean. Something to prevent Father from arresting Jakob. But I didn't think of anything right there. Everything happened so fast and I had to follow Father's orders. I didn't immediately think that I could disobey him." I surprised myself by saying so much to Mr. Wallenberg, seeing as I had just met him. But there was something about him that invited trust. A look of deep understanding and sympathy in his eyes.

"Yes, you were in a very difficult situation. And still are, I suspect," he said, frowning. "I'm very sorry that we weren't successful in also rescuing your friend, Jakob. We tried everything possible. I don't understand why he didn't respond when his name was called." He looked at Brother Ferenc and shook his head, still puzzled.

"Well, I suspect that you're here to see the Vargas, so I won't keep you," Mr. Wallenberg continued. "One of my men can escort you if you like. But the Vargas are still in the same room," he said addressing Brother Ferenc. "Down the hall, on the other side of the building. I'm working on finding a safer, more permanent place for them to live in while they're in hiding. If only I knew which of the buildings were safe from the wrath of the Arrow Cross. They are more troublesome at times than the Nazis."

"Thank you for going through the extra trouble on their behalf," said Brother Ferenc with a small bow of his head. "Yes, we would like to see the Vargas, but you needn't send anyone with us. I know my way to their room by now." He turned to go.

"Mr. Wallenberg," I said, stopping Brother Ferenc in mid stride. "I would like to be of more help. You know that my father is unaware of my involvement in all of this," I waved my arm around to indicate all of what Wallenberg was doing. "Maybe, maybe I can find out where the Arrow Cross plan to go next to make arrests and let you know – or anything else that you think I could help with," I added. "Please, I want to help you save more lives." I took a deep breath. "I want to try to undo what my father is doing,"

My words made me feel horrible, yet I knew I had to say them. I couldn't stand by and let people suffer and die when there was something I could do to help. I refused to let myself think ahead to the consequences that my working against Father would entail. Instead I recalled the haggard faces of the people in the ghetto. I recalled Jakob's face as he looked at me for the last time. I stood up straighter and squared my shoulders, willing Mr. Wallenberg to take me seriously.

He looked at me silently for a long time. Then he looked down at his desk, drummed his fingers on the surface, thinking. I held my breath, hoping that Brother Ferenc wouldn't raise his previous objections to any future involvement on my part.

"You are in a curious position," Mr. Wallenberg said at last, looking back up at me. "What if I suspect that you are actually here to gain information for your father about *our* activities? Or what is to happen if even though you are sympathetic to our cause now, at some point your loyalties shift back to your father? Will you then put our whole operation and the lives of hundreds of hidden people at risk?"

He paused again, his deep brown eyes never wavering from my face. His comment took me by surprise. I hadn't thought of those possibilities, but now I could easily see that given my connection to Father, my presence here could seem highly suspicious. I didn't know how to respond so I said nothing, returning his steady gaze. It was up to Mr. Wallenberg to either believe me or not.

Chapter 22

"I choose to trust you," Mr. Wallenberg said at last. "I can see in your eyes that you are honest and dedicated and that you truly desire to help. You seem like a fine young man and your recent actions regarding the Vargas are a testament of your sincerity. As to what turn events might take in the future, I'm afraid we are all facing uncertainty in that regard. Let's take things one step at a time and do whatever good we can in the present moment." I breathed a sigh of relief at his words, but Mr. Wallenberg held up a cautioning hand.

"At the same time, though what you suggest could prove to be helpful, very helpful indeed, it is also highly dangerous. I'm reluctant to save one life at the risk of losing another. Especially one as young as yours."

"I will be careful," I insisted, "I promise! Father will never suspect a thing. I don't even need to come back here anymore. If I happen to gain some information from Father, I can tell it to Brother Ferenc and he can pass it on to you." I looked at Brother Ferenc hoping he didn't mind that I had suggested further involvement on his part. I needn't have worried.

"I would be most happy to participate in any way you need me to," he said, moving up beside me. "I am of like mind with Ivan. I too would like to do whatever is within my means. I feel like I have stood by long enough, simply wringing my hands in despair at what is unfolding in the city around us. Ivan has breathed new hope into my old bones with his actions and eagerness to help in these rescue efforts." Mr. Wallenberg looked back and forth between us, then at the man sitting at the desk behind him who gave a slight nod of what I hoped was approval.

"Very well," Mr. Wallenberg said turning back to us. "I think you're aware of our operation here. While the Swedish legation's main job is to oversee and assist economic and cultural transactions between Sweden and Hungary, some of us are also secretly involved in procuring Swedish protective documents for Jews. For this we need names and photographs of Jewish citizens, preferably before they are arrested. Unfortunately, the Arrow Cross are not as respectful of these immunity papers as the Nazis. They have been known to tear them up and totally disregard them. Thus, we can be most effective in instances where the arrests are made either by the Nazi soldiers alone or when the two are working together. For now, the Arrow Cross must still follow the Nazi rule.

"Ivan, if you can get us advance information on which of the designated Jewish buildings or which areas of the ghetto will be targeted next, we can try to reach the people in those locations first. Or better yet, if you can get us the actual lists of names, we can create the documents and somehow try to get the accompanying pictures in advance of the arrests. I have a couple of Jewish photographers secretly working here in the building with us. They are good at sneaking snapshots.

"Just remember," he held his hand up again, calming my obvious enthusiasm. "Remember that unfortunately we can't save everyone," he continued. Only a handful or two with each transport. Don't get discouraged. One life saved is better than none. There is a Jewish saying that I have heard repeated often these days: *'whoever saves one life, it is as if he saved the entire world.'*

"Go and see your friends the Vargas now. But I thank you in advance for your anticipated help. Whenever you have something, let Brother Ferenc know." Mr. Wallenberg stretched out to his hand to shake ours. We turned to leave the room. We were almost out the door when Mr. Wallenberg stopped us.

"Ivan, don't forget that in many respects you are still a boy," he said. "Take advantage of it. It doesn't hurt to act childish sometimes. Useful information is often revealed by unsuspecting adults in the presence of children or unwittingly be passed between children themselves." He winked at me, then turned back to the man at the desk.

Chapter 23

Brother Ferenc and I hurried down the hallway in silence. My mind was filled with my conversation with Mr. Wallenberg. I very much wanted to help him in any way I could.

We passed several rooms whose doors stood ajar and the rapid clicking of typewriters and raised voices echoed out into the stone-lined corridor. But many of the doors were also mysteriously shut and I wondered if families like the Vargas were hidden behind them. We turned a corner and Brother Ferenc stopped and knocked on the first door on our right. It was opened within seconds by Mr. Varga.

"Ivan!" he cried as soon as he saw me. He pulled me into the room and embraced me. "Come on in, come in," he said when he had let go. "We are so pleased to see you. We owe you our lives. You were very brave to come and warn us. I am sorry that I ever doubted you." By then, Mrs. Varga had also hurried over and embraced me.

"If only our Jakob could be here with us too," she said through tear filled eyes. Her words shattered the warm glow I felt at Mr. Varga's praise.

"I'm sorry that Mr. Wallenberg couldn't get him back," I said quietly. "He said he doesn't understand why Hendrik, I mean Jakob, wasn't on the train."

"He *was* on the train. I saw him." I turned towards the source of those words, uttered in a deep yet melodious voice. A woman rose from where she had been sitting on a bed against the far wall and came towards us. I immediately recognized her as the woman from the ghetto who, with the young girl had been forced onto the truck with Jakob. She was slightly taller and thinner than Mrs. Varga and her curly, auburn hair had more of a reddish tinge. But her eyes and lips and the general shape of her face bore a strong resemblance to Mrs. Varga's.

Seeing her also brought to my mind the young man who had come to their defense as Father's officers were arresting them. The man who had been shot. He had called this woman 'Mother'.

"This is my sister in-law, Miriam," Mr. Varga introduced us. "You can call her Aunt Mimi as Jakob and pretty much everybody else does. I believe that you saw her in the ghetto. She told us about everything that happened there and the boy who was ordered to notify the guards to arrest us. She and her daughter Lilly were on the train with Jakob, but in a different car from his."

I looked at her and the horror of the whole scene in the ghetto flashed before me once again.

"I'm sorry," I said, feeling my words to be totally inadequate. "I'm so sorry that I couldn't stop what happened in the ghetto."

"It's all right," she said taking my hand in both of hers, "I doubt there's anything you could have done to prevent those brutes from carrying out their mission. But I do want to thank you for your efforts afterwards to get us off the train. If only," her voice broke and her eyes filled with tears, "if only my Gabor could have been saved as well." She let go my hand and wiped the spilled tears off her cheeks. "But I'm grateful that Lilly was spared. At least we have each other." She glanced towards the bed behind her and I saw the young girl from the ghetto huddled there in the corner at the foot of the bed. She had her knees drawn up against her chest and her long straggly hair draped down over her arms. Her face was barely visible, but I could feel the glare of her eyes upon me.

"I do prefer seeing you in your school uniform rather than that Arrow Cross one you had on the other day," Aunt Mimi said with a slight smile.

"And I much prefer wearing it," I confessed. A shudder ran through me at the thought of putting on that now hated uniform again. Yet, if I was to keep up my disguise in front of Father, if I was to help Mr, Wallenberg as I had promised, then wearing it again was inevitable. I pushed the thought aside. I had other things to focus on for now.

"Come and sit down," Mrs. Varga beckoned us towards a small round table in the centre of the room, surrounded by five chairs. One of the chairs was already occupied by Magda their housekeeper. Brother Ferenc and I promptly obeyed her request and Mr. Varga followed us. Aunt Mimi moved back to the bed to sit next to Lilly, pulling the girl up against her side.

"I'm sorry that we can't be more hospitable," Mrs. Varga apologized as she laid some plain rounds of dry rye bread, a bit of cheese and glasses of water on the table. "But the rations here are even more restricted than what we had before. This is all we have to offer."

"You are most kind in offering to share with us the little you have," Brother Ferenc responded. "However, we did not come here to eat but simply to see how you are all faring and to give young Ivan here an opportunity to exchange a few words with you."

"Yes," said Mr. Varga. "I suppose we have some explaining to do. It must have come as quite a shock to you to discover that we are Jewish," he said taking one of the chairs and turning to me. "Especially given the circumstances under which you found out." He shook his head and ran his hand across his forehead.

"I don't know what possessed Jakob to go there – especially without telling us. Such a foolish thing to do."

"I've told you before. Jakob said he needed to know if you did the right thing in pretending to be Catholic," Aunt Mimi interrupted in a bitter tone from the corner. "He wanted to find out about the Jewish faith that you forced him to abandon. He said you always avoided talking about those things. And," she added more quietly, "he wanted to visit us,"

"I suspect that I am partly to blame for that," said Brother Ferenc with a deep sigh. "I had suggested to the boys a couple of weeks ago that as their confirmation approaches, they need to start thinking for themselves about their faith and take responsibility for what they believed and for their own religious formation, for all of their actions. I never dreamt that it would lead to this"

"Yes," I said remembering again that Jakob had looked agitated at the time. "He must have started thinking then about whether or not he wanted to be confirmed in the Catholic faith. I guess for him it was a much more significant decision than for the rest of us boys. It's probably why he decided to visit the ghetto. I had sensed that something was wrong, but I had been too preoccupied with spending the following Saturday with Father to worry about Jakob and what might be bothering him." I hung my head ashamed to admit my own selfish role in the whole thing. "Maybe if I had invited him to come along, or not gone myself, none of this would have happened."

"No, please don't blame yourselves," Mr. Varga said. "If anyone is to blame, it's me. I'm afraid I made a big mistake in not talking with Jakob more about what was happening in the world and about why it was essential to hide our Jewish identity. You see," he said, spreading his hands palm upwards and looking from me to Brother Ferenc, "when I first bought the false identity papers and we moved from our old neighbourhood on the Pest side, and erased our past, and adopted a completely new life, Jakob was only eight years old. He was too young to understand, especially since things here in Hungary weren't that bad yet for the Jews. But after what happened in Germany on Kristallnacht and after my brother-in-law Peter, Aunt Mimi's husband was sent to a labour camp, I suspected that it was only a matter of time until all of Hungary's Jews would also suffer the same fate as so many did in Europe. I took immediate action and paid a very large sum of money to have not only our identities altered but also to be set up with a fine new job and home. It was imperative in my mind that we embrace this new life completely and erase our past!" Mr. Varga stood up and started pacing back and forth in front of us, looking at me every now and then as he spoke as if making sure I understood.

"But, like I said, Jakob was too young to understand. Even some adults couldn't comprehend why I felt it was necessary to take such drastic action." Here I noticed him glance quickly towards Aunt Mimi. "Instead of explaining things fully to Jakob I used my authority as his father to instill fear in him if he ever breathed a word about our past to anyone. It was a matter of life and death, and I made sure he understood that much. And then," he paused and came to stand in front of me, "and then, the very next day after our move, you turned up on our doorstep.

"You, with your father a member of the underground Arrow Cross Party, though I only discovered that after a few days." He sneered when he referred to the Arrow Cross and for an instant my compassion for his plight wavered. I didn't agree with what Father was doing, but I still didn't like to hear other people saying negative things about him. He was my father after all.

"At first I was frightened about your friendship," Mr. Varga continued, oblivious to my momentary resentment. "But after thinking about it, I realized that it could benefit us greatly. What better cover could we have than to be in close relationship with a family aligned with the Arrow Cross? So I encouraged Jakob to be your friend, while at the same time I insisted that he say nothing to you about his past." Mr. Varga hung his head and stopped in front of me.

"For months I quizzed him each night about everything the two of you did and talked about. I plagued him till I think he was too frightened to say anything to me at all. I am so sorry," Mr. Varga ran his fingers through his hair. "I realize now how wrong that was. How it cut off all possibility of open communication between us. No wonder Jakob wouldn't tell me what was going on in his mind, about what he was planning to do." Mr. Varga resumed his pacing.

As he paced, for a few moments saying nothing, I thought about Jakob. How different, yet at the same time, how similar our situations were. We both lived in fear of our fathers. We both hid from each other what we truly thought and felt because of that. If only our friendship could have risen above that fear and we had confided in one another, how different this day would be!

"I should have trusted him more," Mr. Varga continued. "I should have acknowledged that he deserved to know and understand. He and you," he turned towards me and smiled ruefully, "are no longer small children. But I was still frightened. Not because I still thought that he might reveal our secret but because I feared that, like so many others, he might not agree with what I did. That he would not have agreed with my putting the safety and well-being of our immediate family before all else. And at any cost." He glanced at Mrs. Varga and from her towards Aunt Mimi. He sank onto one of the chairs and buried his face in his hands. I could not tell if his next words were muffled by his hands or the sorrow that thickened his voice and trickled tears between his fingers.

"And now, all my plans are ruined, and Jakob is gone. I am so sorry if I did the wrong thing. I am so very, very sorry."

Chapter 24

I squirmed on my seat. I felt uncomfortable at Mr. Varga's emotional expression of regret. I had never seen an adult man cry before. I didn't know what to say or do. I could imagine Father's contempt at this apparent show of weakness. Yet I sensed that it must require a great deal of courage to admit openly that you had made a mistake, to ask for forgiveness. I wondered if Father would ever be able to do that.

"Do not judge yourself too harshly, my son," Brother Ferenc said quietly, coming over and laying a hand on Mr. Varga's shoulder. "You must look forward. Be thankful that you have the opportunity to do what is right from now on."

"But Jakob is gone!" Mr. Varga exclaimed and stood up so suddenly that he knocked his chair over. He faced Brother Ferenc. "Jakob is gone!" he repeated, "taken to who knows where. How can I right that?"

"Janos," Mrs. Varga stepped between the two men and gripped Mr. Varga's arms. "Please, Brother Ferenc is right. We can't waste time worrying about what we should have done differently. Maybe there is something we can do now to get Jakob back. We have to focus on that and on how to survive so that we are here for him when he returns." Though her voice trembled, she calmed Mr. Varga with her steady gaze.

"At least you know he's not dead," Aunt Mimi spoke up from the corner, her deep voice still tinged with bitterness. "At least there is hope that you can still get *him* back. That's more than I can say for my Gabor."

Again, I felt terrible seeing the pain and sorrow of these adults around me. And I felt guilty because my parents were both Arrow Cross members, the group responsible for all this suffering and anguish. Aunt Mimi had seen her son murdered just a few days ago. Looking forward wouldn't be that easy for her. Yet, at the same time I felt that she was being somewhat harsh. Her words hurt Mr. Varga who had said that he was sorry for how he had acted in the past. Not just regarding Jakob, but regarding the whole family. I wished that she was a bit more understanding, more forgiving, kinder. I felt bad for Mr. Varga who needed her compassion more than anyone else's.

I looked at the girl huddled next to Aunt Mimi. Lilly. She had stirred at her mother's words and now her features were more visible. Dark, deep set eyes, a thin face with a pointed chin. I remembered how thin and fragile she had seemed in the ghetto. For some reason I felt particularly protective of her and experienced a surge of satisfaction in the role I had played in getting her off the train. She would never have survived the journey, let alone the horrors that Father had described of camp life.

"I think we had best get going now," Brother Ferenc's voice broke the uncomfortable silence that had followed Aunt Mimi's comment. "I will let you know promptly if Ivan gains any useful information from his father about what has happened to Jakob."

"Yes," Mrs. Varga hurried over to me and embraced me. "You are our closest tie to Jakob now. I thank you again for what you have done for us already. Please come back and see us again if that is possible."

I tried to think of something positive to say but looking into Mrs. Varga's sorrow filled eyes, I was reluctant to make any promises that I could not keep. But I knew that she wanted to hear at least a few positive, hopeful words. Then I remembered the box.

"I went to your apartment and took a few things," I said. "They're just small things that I thought you might like to have as a reminder. That might mean something to you. I didn't really know what you'd want, but I wanted to grab some things for you before…," I stopped abruptly realizing what I was about to say. *'Before your apartment is looted by the Nazis and Arrow Cross. By my own mother and father.'*

"It's alright," Mrs. Varga said. "I understand. We know what happens to the belongings of Jews who disappear. That is the least of our worries now. But thank you for thinking of doing that for us. It will be nice to have a reminder of what our past lives had been like. It is a life we can never go back to now. If we survive all this," she added.

Chapter 25

"Have you had any news about Hendrik?" I asked Father that evening as we sat at the dinner table. "I mean, do you know where he is? If he arrived at that – that camp?"

"Your little 'once upon a time' friend is probably getting his first taste of life at Auschwitz. He's probably had his head shaved and been branded with his prisoner's number by now. Maybe he has even had his first taste of camp fare. We'll see how long he survives on that," Father said, waving a large chunk of sausage speared on the end of his fork at me.

Because Father was a member of the Arrow Cross, we had special privileges when it came to food. The rest of the country lived according to their ration card allotments. One egg a day for a family, meat maybe once or twice a week if someone was lucky, a loaf of rye bread if there were any left at the bakery when it was finally your turn after waiting in line for hours. It all depended on how important you were to the officials.

But people like Father were often given extra rations to take home from the supplies brought into the city for the German troops. When Mother went to the butcher's shop or the grocers, the waiting people would make way for her and let her go to the front of the line. Once inside, owners usually had something special saved for her. Everyone wanted to be on good terms with the family of an Arrow Cross officer. The rest of Budapest's population learned to live frugally.

"No more fancy meals for Hendrik, I'm afraid," Father added with a chuckle.

"And to think that I often shared our extra supplies with those liars!" Mother said with indignation.

"Not that I know anything specific about him," Father continued ignoring Mother's outburst. "Once the prisoners get to those camps only the SS and other Nazi officials are in charge. We have nothing more to do with them. But I've heard the rumors," he said with a wink. I hoped Father didn't notice the shudder that passed through me at his words. This was not the kind of information I was going to tell the Vargas.

"By the way," Father continued after he swallowed his next bite of meat, "how would you like to accompany me again on Saturday? We won't be in the Ghetto. This time, I'll be in charge of collecting prisoners from some of the Jewish designated buildings."

I almost said that I couldn't go. That I had a big assignment to finish for school. I never wanted to wear an Arrow Cross uniform again or be a witness and silent accomplice to what the soldiers did. But then I remembered about my promise to Mr. Wallenberg. This was my chance to find out where the Arrow Cross were going to be arresting Jews. If I went along, I might even have an opportunity to save some lives of people who couldn't get protection papers from Mr. Wallenberg. My heart pounded with excitement at the prospect.

"Yes, of course! I would love to come!" I said, glad that I didn't have to fake my enthusiasm. "Which streets will we be going to?" Father smiled and pulled a small brown leather-bound notebook out of his pocket. He flipped through the pages.

"Let me see," he said. "On Saturday we will be on Korona St. There are several yellow star buildings there." I repeated the street name several times in my head, though I was sure I would not forget it. Before classes even started tomorrow morning, I would get the information to Brother Ferenc.

"With the blasted Russians advancing on our borders," Father continued in a grim tone, "we are stepping up our efforts to transport as many Jews as possible to the camps. The trains are starting to have a hard time reaching their destination, often detouring around enemy troops, sometimes they even have to turn back. The Nazis have started marching the prisoners to the camps. If things continue like this, we may have to resort to eliminating Jews right here. Soon they may be facing our own firing squad."

"A firing squad?" I asked not sure if I understood correctly. "You mean they'll be shot right here in the city?" It would mean a quicker, more certain death; less opportunity to rescue people from a slowly moving train. No hope of somehow surviving the hardships of a camp.

"Yes," Father nodded with a satisfied air. "We plan to line them up along the banks of the Danube for all to see. We're not going to let the Russians or Americans stop us from our goal." Then, after a moment of silent pondering Father added, "Perhaps it's time you learned how to shoot a rifle with real bullets."

Chapter 26

Thursday, Nov 10

I had a hard time getting to sleep that night. I tossed and turned as my emotions switched back and forth between excitement and apprehension. Excitement that I had something valuable to report to Mr. Wallenberg so soon and apprehension over what the coming Saturday would bring.

Also, there was the overwhelming guilt and fear about working secretly against my father.

Several times I jumped out of bed, determined to go to Father in his study, where I knew he would be still filling out forms and writing notes. Again, I debated about confessing everything I had done. Telling him how I felt about the Arrow Cross and the way the Jews were treated. I wanted to be open and honest with him as I used to be. I didn't understand how he could be tied up with a cause that was so clearly wrong. How could he not see and feel the pain of the people whose lives he was destroying? I remembered the pang of guilt on account of my father back in the Varga's room at the Swedish Legation building. I didn't want to feel that way about Father. I wanted to be proud of him and to look up to him like I had as a young child. Surely, we could talk and he would understand.

But each time I reached my bedroom door and placed my hand on the doorknob, I hesitated and turned back. Father's views were not to be challenged. I had learned that well at an early age. Plus, if I told Father everything and he disagreed with me and remained firm in his commitment to the Arrow Cross, then I would be endangering the lives of the very people I had just helped to save as well as the lives of many others. I could not take that chance.

I buried my face in my pillow. I thought of Brother Ferenc at the Franciscan monastery. He had hinted that some of his fellow monks didn't understand the wrongness of what was happening, that he had to hide his activities from them. How did he manage to remain so calm and serene in their midst and live harmoniously with them, and still do whatever he could to help the Jews? I finally decided to ask his advice before saying anything to Father. I hoped there would be time for that the next day when I passed on the information about the upcoming activities of the Arrow Cross on Saturday.

After that, I finally fell into a fitful sleep.

I arrived early at school the next morning in the hopes of talking with Brother Ferenc before classes started. As I approached the building, I noticed Zoltan leaning against the large Chestnut tree whose massive branches overshadowed the front steps. He seemed to be waiting for me. Two other boys, close to him in size and whom I recognized from the school soccer team, stepped out from behind the tree and barred my way.

"Hey," Zoltan said, "I saw you leaving with Brother Ferenc yesterday. The two of you seemed to be in quite a hurry. What was so important that you missed the Levente meeting? You never turned up yesterday. Not even late. Was good old 'Friar Tuck' dragging you to the police for attacking me or is he in league with you in protecting the Jews?"

"It's none of your business what I do or with whom," I said, trying to push past him.

"It is so my business," he retorted pushing back at me. "It's against the law to help Jews in any way. It's my duty to report you if you're secretly hiding your friend's parents somewhere."

"I'm not hiding them!" I said angrily, hoping that I sounded convincing. "I have no idea where they are. And don't think you're so important that Brother Ferenc would waste his time over that insignificant incident in the dining room. He was just taking me to the apartment of an elderly couple who needed some furniture moved. In the Levente we're encouraged to serve our comrades in need. It was good physical labour that I'm sure will be approved. So mind your own business!" I surprised myself by how readily I had taken to lying. I had always thought of lying as dishonorable. But right now, it was telling the truth that would have been wrong, dishonorable to people who needed protection. I didn't have time to waste over such scruples.

"It's true," a voice said over my right shoulder. I turned and noticed that Tibor, who was in my class and who sometimes joined Jakob and me in a game of soccer at the park, had come up behind me. Obviously he had overheard my brief exchange with Zoltan. "They happened to come to the same building where I have my piano lesson. I saw them there," he said. I was surprised to hear this obvious lie told in my defense. We instantly became partners in deception. I smiled gratefully at Tibor and then turned back to Zoltan

"And if you're so worried about whether or not I'm working against my father, why don't you come to Korona Street on Saturday and see what you think after that," I said with renewed defiance. I hoped that once Zoltan saw me in an Arrow Cross uniform his suspicions would disappear. "Helping the Arrow Cross counts for more than turning up for Levente training," I added. "Isn't your father with the Arrow Cross as well? I haven't heard of you joining him in any activities."

I stepped around Zoltan and his buddies who made no move to stop me this time. Tibor followed and we went into the school building.

"Thank you," I said as the doors closed behind us. "Zoltan's just a bully."

"I agree," Tibor said. "I don't like the way he pushes others around. With everything going on out there," Tibor waved his arm towards the door, "the more people like him that we stop at this stage, the better." I looked at Tibor with curiosity. Did he feel the same as me? Could I trust him?

"My father's a journalist,' he said when he saw me hesitate, "He was reporting on the scene outside the Swedish Legation building yesterday when he noticed Brother Ferenc entering through a side door with a student who I now assume was you. Father mentioned it at supper last night. I didn't think much of it until I overheard your conversation with Zoltan just now." He paused and as if suspecting my doubts about how much I could trust him, he laid a hand on my shoulder and leaning close, whispered in my ear. "It's alright, relax, I'm on your side." I looked into his eyes in wonder. How much did he know or guess? What exactly did he mean by being on my side?

"I know a bit about the Swedish Legation and what they are trying to do there for the Jews," Tibor continued, still trying to reassure me. "I figure that if you went there with Brother Ferenc, then you must be trying to help too. My father is. Helping that is. He tells the rest of the world the truth of what is happening here. Secretly of course." Tibor smiled. His words lifted a great load off my shoulders. I was no longer alone with my burden. While I had the help and support of Brother Ferenc, being able to share things with someone my own age made a huge difference. I smiled gratefully in return at Tibor.

Having always had Hendrik as my constant and close companion, I hadn't spent much time developing deep friendships with the other boys at the school. Especially, I hadn't given much attention to Tibor who was smaller in build from us and apart from joining in the occasional soccer game at the park, didn't appear to be overly interested in sports and fitness. Not like Hendrik and me. It's not that I thought of him as weak, I simply hadn't thought of him at all.

But now I saw Tibor truly for the first time and realized that there were other ways of being strong than just physically.

"I have to go and see Brother Ferenc right now," I said, "but let's sit together at lunch, somewhere out of the way in the dining room, where we can talk." Tibor nodded in agreement as I hurried off.

Chapter 27

I found Brother Ferenc in his office. I relayed the information I had learned from Father to him and with a pleased tone he assured me that he would pass it on.

"I think that this is exactly the kind of help that Mr. Wallenberg had hoped you could provide him with. Good work Ivan," he said.

Elated by his response and with the prospect of talking with Tibor at lunch time, I almost forgot my personal conflict that I had wanted to talk to Brother Ferenc about. I had my hand on the door handle when my scruples of the previous night came flooding back.

"Brother Ferenc," I cleared my throat as I turned back to face him, "there's something else. I – I'd like to ask you about something."

"Of course, Ivan," he said stepping back and indicating that I should have a seat.

"It's about Father," I began once we were both seated, facing each other. "I – I don't know what to do." Hesitantly at first, I poured out my anxieties over deceiving Father as well as my longing to once again see him in the same light as I had just a few weeks ago. A father who I could trust and look up to. A father I loved.

Brother Ferenc listened, then remained silent for a long moment after I had finished. He thoughtfully fingered the frayed tassel of the thick, twisted cord that served as a belt for his cassock.

"You are in a difficult position indeed, and I'm sorry that you have to live through times like this." He sighed, then continued. "You were wise to refrain from speaking with your father last night. He has been with the Arrow Cross for many years and has held his views regarding the Jews, the Gypsies and people who deviate from the norm in any way, for even longer. I don't know his history or what influences in his past has brought him to this state of mind. I do know that people wiser and more influential than you or I have tried to sway your father's views without success. As his son it is not your job to educate or correct your father. Not yet at any rate." He paused.   The school bells announcing the start of classes shattered the silence. Brother Ferenc waved the intrusion aside.

"Let's ignore that for the moment," he said. "I am free from teaching for the first hour today. I will give you a late slip to give to your teacher."

"For now," Brother Ferenc said, resuming his previous train of thought, "remember that your silence and vigilant observation at home is helping to save lives. It may not seem like much, but it is the most important and courageous thing you can do right now."

"What about Saturday?" I asked. "Do you think I should try to get out of that? I can't stand the thought of anyone thinking that I've become one of the Arrow Cross." But suddenly, as soon as I said that, I remembered my taunting words to Zoltan just minutes ago. I realized that I couldn't back out of going. For what if he went, and I wasn't there as I said I would be?

"I know that accompanying your father on Saturday will be difficult," Brother Ferenc replied without being aware of the thoughts that just coursed through my mind. "But who knows, maybe there will be some small things you can do to secretly ease the suffering of the people being rounded up. Remember the difference that your presence made last Saturday. Think of the lives that would be lost now if you hadn't been there." I nodded, recognizing the truth of his words. No matter how uncomfortable, I would be at my father's side on Saturday.

"As for your father," Brother Ferenc continued, "in many respects, he is a good man. He loves you and your mother and provides for all your needs. He is making sure that you get the best education possible. When you are with him, try to focus on what is good in him. Respond to that. Despite his failings, try to love the good that is there. That is what God does with all of us, for none of us are perfect."

I closed my eyes for a moment. I felt again the shock at witnessing the anger and hatred on my father's face when he dealt with the Jews in the ghetto, when he confronted Jakob.

But then, prompted by Brother Ferenc's words, I recalled Father laughing as he spread a lavish feast out on our picnic blanket near the end of the summer - a time when food was already being rationed and becoming scarce for many. I saw in my mind the joy on his face when he gave me a new bike on my birthday, the pride he showed when I beat him at a short sprint for the first time. My eyes filled with tears. Brother Ferenc was right. Father was not all bad.

"Thank you," I said, barely above a whisper. "I will try to do that."

"Good," said Brother Ferenc, "but don't be deceived. It's not going to be easy. You can always take comfort in the knowledge that you do have a Father who is perfect and who loves you with a divine love. Pray to Him for guidance."

Chapter 28

Sitting in a deep window alcove of the dining room, partially concealed behind a tall ornamental sideboard, and balancing plates of food on our drawn-up knees, Tibor and I faced each other.

"So," Tibor began, carefully choosing his words, "like Zoltan, I too assume that since Hendrik was your best friend you had known all along that he is Jewish and that it didn't matter to you. I mean," he frowned as if thinking it through as he spoke, "clearly your parents, especially your father couldn't have known. Everyone knows that your father belongs to the Arrow Cross. But," he said, holding up his hand to ward off an interruption from me, "unlike Zoltan, I don't care that Hendrik is Jewish and that you helped him to keep it a secret. In fact, I admire you for it.

"After I figured out this morning that it was you at the Swedish Legation building with Brother

Ferenc, and knowing, through my father that they are trying to protect some of the Jewish population, I figure that perhaps you too are actually trying to help in some way? Is it because of Hendrik? Is that where his family is now? Or is there more to it?"

Still not sure just how much I could trust Tibor, I too chose my words carefully.

"You're wrong in your first assumption that I knew all along that Hendrik is Jewish. I didn't. I only found that out last Saturday, same as my father and everyone else." I saw the surprise on Tibor's face at my statement, but he remained silent, allowing me to continue. "At the same time, you're right in that it doesn't matter to me whether Hendrik is Jewish or not. He's my friend. I know what he's like as a person. What difference does his religion make?" I frowned, attempting to honestly sort through my feelings for the first time.

"I admit that as soon as the reality of what he said registered, I was disappointed for a moment. Why hadn't he trusted me? We were best friends!" The pain of that moment of realization stabbed me again.

"But then, almost immediately," I continued, wanting to explain not only to Tibor but also to myself, "I realized that of course Hendrik couldn't take any chances. Not when his life and the life of his family depended on him keeping their secret. No matter how much he trusted me." I recalled those conversations concerning the treatment of the Jews and in my mind, saw for the first time, Hendrik's guarded look. How he often changed the subject if I happened to refer to Father's authority on the subject.

"He knew how much I admired and feared my father," I said, suddenly ashamed of how blind I had been. "My father, the Arrow Cross Sargeant, who with just a nod of his head can have someone killed on the spot." I thought of the scene in the ghetto. Of Hendrik's cousin dropping to the ground and the blood pooling out from beneath him. "What if, even unintentionally, I blurted out Hendrik's secret? Given how Jews are being treated in Hungary, it was unthinkable!"

Tibor leaned forward and gripped my arm with his hand. His hand which, though so much smaller than mine, felt surprisingly strong.

"Hendrik must have understood that you wouldn't knowingly oppose your father. Not back then," he said. I wondered just how much Tibor guessed or suspected about my involvement with the disappearance of the Varga family. A moment ago, he had asked if they were hiding at the Swedish Embassy. I had managed not to answer that specific question and hoped to avoid saying anything further about them. To my relief, Tibor changed the subject.

"You had mentioned something to Zoltan about going to Korona Street on Saturday. What was that about?" he asked.

"My father is taking me with him on Saturday to help with the rounding up of Jews on Korona Street."

"You're kidding!" said Tibor, wide eyed. "How can you do that? Are you actually going with him to help? I thought you just said…" I held up my hand to stop Tibor.

"Yes, I'm going with him," I said cutting Tibor off in mid-sentence, impatient for him to understand. "I have to. I can't let my father find out that I'm not on his side. If he does then I can't be of help to – to people like Hendrik's family." I stumbled over the last words. "But, though I'm going with my father, I'm hoping that I can avoid actually participating in the round-up. Maybe, somehow," I added recalling Brother Ferenc's words, "I can even secretly try to save some of the people."

"Really?" Tibor asked, once again his eyes wide with astonishment, "Do you really think that you can be of help? I wish that I could be a part of that! Do you think I could come with you?"

I shook my head. "I couldn't ask Father. Though it would be wonderful to have a friend with me. I wish you could've seen what it's like inside the ghetto. I hope the conditions in the Jewish buildings are better. I just hope nobody gets shot this time." I described to Tibor about how we had come upon Hendrik and learned that his name was really Jakob. I described the arrest and how the young man was shot. But still, I made no mention of what I did afterwards.

"Wow!" he said as I finished. "All of that must have been horrible to witness." I nodded. It was a relief to be able to talk to someone my own age about all of this. Someone who felt as I did.

"I have a secret to tell you," Tibor said, leaning towards me and lowering his voice to a whisper.

"My Aunt Szilvi has a small grocery store on Sandor Street. My mother helps her out there part time. Well, there is a cellar beneath the length of the store and they are hiding some Jewish women and their young children down there. Aunt Szilvi plays gypsy music all day long on an old gramophone in order to drown out the sound of children crying or playing. She says you can't expect children to be silent all day. If her customers grumble about the volume of the music, she tells them she prefers it to hearing the noise from the tanks and planes and guns all day long."

I was shocked to hear Tibor reveal this secret to me so readily.

"Should you have told me that? How do you know I won't tell my father?" He looked at me for a long moment in silence.

"Because I know you wouldn't," he said at last, leaning back. "Not after all you've just said. And obviously Brother Ferenc trusts you since he took you with him to the Swedish Legation. Besides, it's nice to finally have someone my own age that I know I can be honest with. I hated having to keep everything to myself all this time."

"I know," I agreed, "I feel the same way. It's great to be able to talk with you about what's going on. So, you haven't told anyone else?"

"No," he shook his head. "It was really tough, but I haven't dared breathe a word to anyone until now."

"Good. Listen," I said, reconsidering, "I'll think about Saturday. I'll try to find out some more information from my father and if there's any way I can think of for you to come, I'll let you know.

"And," I added before we parted, "since we know that Hendrik's real name is Jakob, let's call him that from now on between us. I think he would like that. I already try to even think of him as Jakob."

"Yes!" Tibor agreed.

Chapter 29

Saturday, Nov. 12

Once again it was Saturday. Once again, I was fastening the buttons on my Arrow Cross uniform and adjusting the collar in front of my mirror. My hands shook. I was filled with apprehension about the coming day. How was I going to live up to Father's expectations while at the same time trying not to hurt people? Would I really be able to save some lives? Would I be able to keep Father from discovering what I was hoping to do behind his back?

The previous day, on Friday, Tibor and I had had our lunch together again in our secluded spot behind the sideboard.

"Isn't it frightening to be working against your own father?" he had asked as we talked again about my upcoming day with Father.

"Yes," I had replied, "but knowing that I might be helping to save people's lives, helps.

"But how? How will you be able to do that?" I had no answer.

As it turned out, it was Brother Ferenc who had come up with a tentative plan for the day.

Tibor and I had gone together to see him at the end of the school day. We wanted to let him know that Tibor too, wanted to help in any way possible to protect the Jews. To our surprise, we discovered that Brother Ferenc was already aware of what Tibor's aunt and parents were doing.

"Your father is a very brave man," he told Tibor. "Every day he risks his life to report secretly to the outside world what is happening here. Finally, other countries are learning the truth of what the Nazis are up to. I assume that he approves of your intention to follow in his footsteps?"

"Yes, sir." Tibor said, sitting up a little bit straighter. "Though I'm to tell him whatever I'm doing so that he can make sure that it's not too dangerous. He said he's not prepared for me to risk my life, just yet."

Brother Ferenc bowed his head in approval, then sat quietly, with his eyes closed for so long, that I began to think that he had dozed off. But then, his eyes opened and he smiled at us.

"Yes," he said, rubbing his hands together. "Everything seems to be falling into place. The Lord is on our side." He leaned towards us and continued.

"Thanks to the information you supplied, Ivan," Brother Ferenc nodded towards me, "Mr. Wallenberg has created false documents and removed a few people from the yellow starred, Jewish buildings on Korona Street to one of his 'safe houses'." I felt a sudden rush of pride at his words. I had managed to help some people! And without arousing Father's suspicion! Perhaps this wasn't going to be so difficult after all. But I couldn't dwell in this glow of satisfaction as Brother Ferenc hurried on.

"Knowing that he couldn't save many," Brother Ferenc was saying, "Wallenberg focused on women with infants and the elderly. They are the ones most at risk of being killed as soon as they get to a camp. Or of dying on route. He regretted that he didn't have time to save more.

"But now, I have a plan," he said with a twinkle in his eyes. "Together, we might be able to rescue some people at the last minute." Tibor and I glanced at one another. Suddenly, Brother Ferenc no longer seemed like the elderly friar that he was. He had become more like one of us. "Every Saturday, we Franciscans take soup to the poor and infirm people throughout the city, to those whose plight has been made known to us," he began.

"Two of the brothers from our house are usually assigned to this task. One drives an old wagon pulled by our humble friend the mule, and the other ladles out the soup from the large wooden caskets on the wagon into smaller containers when we get to our various destinations. I have volunteered to be the driver tomorrow for our brother house across the river. It is a house which is not far from Korona Street, located near a poorer neighbourhood and where the brothers are always shorthanded for this task. I suggested that it be one of our boys who accompanies me on my rounds,"

"Me!" Tibor interrupted, jumping out of his chair. "That would be me!"

" – for the edification of his soul," Brother Ferenc continued. "My suggestion has been approved. And yes, I am hoping that you will be that boy, Tibor," he smiled at Tibor who stood beaming. Brother Ferenc straightened up and turned to me.

"Now then Ivan," he said, "my plan is to meander with my wagon through that district of the city until I reach the alley behind Korona Street. By then several of my barrels should be empty. If by some chance you could manage to secretly direct some the residents, those who are designated to be deported, out into the alley, Tibor and I will do our best to collect them, hide them in or around the barrels and transport them to one of Mr. Wallenberg's safe houses." Brother Ferenc sat back, folded his arms across his chest and looked at us. "It will be risky work, for none of the soldiers can suspect what you are doing. Do you think you can manage that?" he asked.

"But when you drive out from the alley into the street, won't the soldiers notice the people on the wagon? Won't you be stopped immediately and arrested as well?" I asked instead of answering

"Ah," Brother Ferenc said reaching up to scratch his short beard, "I forgot to mention that the wagon has a large brown canvas tarp covering the barrels. In case of rain, you know. There should be room for several people to hide beneath it among the barrels. Also, I will ensure that the two barrels at the back of the wagon always have some soup in them so that if I get stopped, I can pull the tarp back partway and show the guards that indeed I am merely transporting food to the hungry."

"If there are children among those rescued, they might make a noise or cry," said Tibor. I guessed he was recalling his aunt's attempts to drown out the hidden children's sounds with music.

"We-ell," said Brother Ferenc chuckling, "maybe you will have to act more childish than you really are and pretend to be making whatever noise is coming from beneath the tarp. But hopefully we can convince any youngsters to be very still and quiet for just a few minutes. Most children these days have had plenty of practice doing that."

"By the way," Brother Ferenc added, still speaking to Tibor. "I understand that your father might be there as well on Korona Street tomorrow. He has an assignment from the Harc (War) newspaper to report on the *heroic* service of the Arrow Cross. At the same time though, he will be trying to snap shots of their brutality for the underground 'Nepszava' (The National Voice) paper. Let's hope both our missions will be successful."

———

"Ivan!"

My father's sharp, commanding voice brought me out of my reflections into the present moment.

"It's time for us to go!" he said. I straightened my tie and hurried to meet him at the front door.

Chapter 30

My apprehension about the upcoming day vanished momentarily as I sat next to my father in the front seat of an army Jeep. We were exposed to the elements, but the day, though cold, was sunny. The speed of the vehicle as we rumbled down the hillside swerving around potholes and sharp corners gave a sense of heightened adventure to our mission.

I gripped the barrel of my father's gun, its stock secured between my knees, trying to keep it and myself from bouncing out into the street. I was not afraid, knowing that as always, Father was in full control. Looking at his laughing face, it was easy to forget what lay ahead. We whooped in unison as the Jeep flew over a short, steep rise in the road.

Soon enough though, we arrived at the ramparts bordering the Danube River. Here our progress was slowed considerably by heavier traffic. We drove across Chain Bridge to the Pest side and into the heart of the always busy center town. The destruction wrought by the nightly air raids was much more severe here than in Buda.

Tibor had told me that his father had access to forbidden, foreign newspapers which in recent days had reported that Russia's Red Army together with the other Allied forces was beating back the German troops. They had crossed the Hungarian border and were slowly advancing towards Budapest. Nightly, Allied planes flew over the city, dropping missiles aiming to destroy Nazi and Arrow Cross headquarters and battalions. From the ground, the Hungarian and German troops fired back at the planes. The fighting was getting more and more intense. I was thankful that we lived on the relatively secluded side of Sas Mountain. Though the building sometimes trembled from nearby bombings, our immediate district had so far escaped direct attack.

As soon as we turned on to Korona Street, the real purpose of the day came rushing back. Several other military vehicles were already lined up along the curb. The soldiers, both German Nazis and Arrow Cross, were standing nearby, smoking cigarettes and stomping their feet in an attempt to warm up. Father and I joined them and after a few greetings and friendly acknowledgments of my presence, I was, to my relief, largely ignored.

I carefully looked up and down the street wondering if I might glimpse Brother Ferenc and Tibor with their wagon making their way towards the back alley. But of course, it was too early for that. Brother Ferenc had a number of soup deliveries to make first and their journey with a mule drawn wagon would be slow and tedious. It occurred to me that they probably wouldn't arrive in this district until well into the afternoon. What would I do if I managed to send some people to the alley before the soup wagon was in place?

I needn't have worried. We stood around for what seemed like hours, before an official looking vehicle, like the Volkswagen I had gotten a ride in last Saturday, arrived and a Nazi officer got out holding a thick sheaf of papers. The men gathered around him and an argument began in mixed German and Hungarian about how to proceed.

From the occasional words and phrases I caught, I gathered that the German Nazis wanted to proceed in an orderly, selective way, arresting only those whose names were on their list for the day. Apparently, some Jews were more important prisoners than others. The Arrow Cross soldiers on the other hand wanted to rid each building completely of its Jewish population.

"What's the point of taking some here and there," I heard one of my father's men grumble. "We're going to kill them all eventually."

As I waited a short distance away, I noticed that the street was unusually quiet. There were no casual pedestrians about or shoppers hurrying to buy some needed item or other. The stores housed on the ground floor of some of the buildings, though open, had no customers coming and going from them. It was then that I remembered that Father had told me that there was a special curfew for Jews, allowing them to leave their buildings only between certain hours in the afternoon. I looked up at the building I was standing in front of, an ancient six story stone structure. A curtain shifted slightly in one recessed window. In another I saw two curious, childish faces gazing down at us before they were ushered away by a protective arm.

I tried to imagine what it must be like to be those people, waiting anxiously to learn who would or would not survive this day. I wished that I could somehow let them know that I was not a part of this. That I was here to try to help them. But I was wearing an Arrow Cross uniform. In appearance at least, I was one of the enemy. I would never be believed, let alone trusted. Will they even listen to me if I tried to direct them to the back alley? Suddenly our plan seemed very foolish.

It was as we prepared to enter the first building that another military Volkswagen drove up. An Arrow Cross officer got out of the driver's side and a boy about my age from the passenger side of the vehicle. He too wore the Arrow Cross uniform. He turned slowly and to my horror I realized that it was Zoltan.

"I bet you didn't think that I would take your suggestion seriously, did you?" he sneered, as he sauntered over to me. "You're not the only one whose father is a bigshot in the Arrow Cross."

Chapter 31

As we entered the first building, Father ordered me to stay by his side and simply observe for now. His instructions were short and clipped as they were with all his men. To my relief, Zoltan too was ordered to stay with his father who, with a few men, mounted the stairs to the top floor of the building while we began going door to door on the ground floor. With a frown, Father studied the document he was handed by the SS guard.

"Why can't they just let us do things our way," I heard him mutter. "It's our country after all."

The first door Father pounded his fist on led to what had once been a small shoe repair shop. It was now occupied by about 10 people huddled around a table at the back. Father shouted a couple of names into the room and two people stepped forward. An elderly man and woman.

"Into the courtyard!" he ordered, punctuating his command with a wave of his rifle. With downcast eyes the couple shuffled to the door, grabbed their overcoats off a hook and went out into the open square where SS guards stood with drawn rifles. We proceeded like this from one residence to the next, sometimes ordering everyone from inside the apartment into the courtyard and sometimes only a few of the occupants. Some of the people went meekly like the first couple while others wailed or objected and sometimes even outright refused. Any resistors were met with threats and beatings by the uniformed guards until they complied. I hung back as much as possible in the hopes of remaining invisible. I knew that I was being of no help to anyone this way, but there was nothing I could do, I told myself. Again, I saw the absurd naiveté of our plan.

It was in one of the units on the second floor, that a young woman, standing straight and defiant, balancing a baby on her hip and a toddler clutching at her skirt, produced a document saying that her family was under Swedish protection and were waiting to be transported out of the country. Father grabbed the document from her hands and with a scowl showed it to the SS guard who accompanied him. The guard studied the document closely then with a curt nod handed it back to the woman.

"Let her be," he said in broken Hungarian to my father.

"What do you mean?" Father demanded. "Her name is on the list."

"Not anymore," the SS guard replied.

"This is ridiculous!" Father objected, "That document is false. A forgery. She's a Jew like the rest. She must go with them."

"She may be a Jew, but it says here that she is also under Swedish protection. We Germans respect that. We are the authority here!" the SS officer put special emphasis on his last words. Father had no option but to obey. I was pleased to witness firsthand the success of Mr. Wallenberg's work.

Once everyone from the lists was gathered in the courtyard of the building, they were herded outside and told to wait in the street under heavily armed guards. If anyone dared to step out of line or object in any way, they were beaten back into place with clubs and rifle butts. Thankfully no one had been shot at yet.

As Zoltan and his father descended the stairs following their ragged line of prisoners, I noticed that unlike me, Zoltan took an active part with his own club in driving the people downwards and then out into the street. Several stumbled and cried out in pain from his blows.

Father must have noticed too and maybe regretted telling me to be a mere observer. As we came abreast of our Jeep on our way to the next building that displayed the yellow star, Father stopped. He opened the trunk and pulled out a rifle.

"It's not loaded," he whispered as he handed it to me, "but no one will know, and it will give you an air of authority. Use it to your advantage."

I followed my father, with a heart as heavy as the rifle in my hands. What was I to do? How was I expected to use it to my advantage? And how much would it further thwart any chance I had to help someone escape?

———

The noon hour had passed, but we did not stop to eat. We entered yet another building and once again split into groups and knocked on the doors marked on the list in my father's hand. Again, the people whose names were called assembled in the courtyard. I had pretty much given up on being able to help anyone at all. Overcome with shame and guilt, I tried not to meet anyone's eyes. Yet I noticed several scornful glances directed towards me – especially by the women.

At first, I wondered why I would attract their ire more than any of the other uniformed Arrow Cross. It was when I saw one of the women pull a boy about my age, protectively closer to herself as they passed by me and my drawn rifle, that I realized that it was probably my youth that made them especially resentful of my presence.

This time there were five people scratched off the list because they had Swedish protection papers. There were several others from the list who were not present.

"Where are these missing people?" Father demanded from no one in particular. He waved his list of names in the air. No one answered.

"Where are they?" he shouted again, reading the names out loud. He dragged an elderly man by his collar from the group.

"I, I don't know," the man cowered on the cobblestones, his arms up over his head to ward off any potential blows.

"You," my father pointed his gun at a woman about Mother's age. "Do you know where they are?"

"They are children," the woman said, her eyes wide with fear. "They must have gone off somewhere to play."

"Gone off somewhere to play?" Father repeated with a sneer. "You think I would fall for that? There's a curfew for pigs like you. They're not allowed to leave the building"

"Please," the woman begged, "they are children. They don't understand about curfews. We try, but every so often they just don't listen."

Father was about to accost someone else, but an SS officer came up to him and said it was time to move the prisoners out.

"We are not ready!" Father retorted.

"That is too bad," the SS officer said in a condescending tone. "We do have other buildings to visit today. Perhaps you can find some other way to deal with your problems here. Some way that won't hold up our operation." And with that, he turned and left. For a moment I felt bad for Father as he flushed, then looked around for a solution to his problem.

As in the ghetto, his eyes came to rest on me.

"Ivan!" he commanded. "Go. Search the cellars! It's the only place we haven't been. I'll send some men back in a few minutes to see if you've found anything." Then he and the soldiers marched the prisoners out of the courtyard.

I stood there, conscious of the eyes of the other officers and especially of Zoltan on me. With feigned confidence, I gripped my rifle as I had seen the soldiers do and strode toward the back stairway leading to the building's cellar.

Chapter 32

Once out of sight, I leapt down the ancient stone steps two and three at a time. The stairwell was dark, narrow, and winding and I almost stumbled a couple of times. I had to hurry. If there were indeed children playing down here, this was my opportunity to save them.

Like many of the other old buildings in this part of the city, the cellar was divided into several compartments where the tenants stored coal during the winter months. Once my eyes adjusted to the dim light, it was easy to see through their cage like walls and determine that there was no one hiding in any of them.

Disappointed, I was about to turn and go back up the stairs when I noticed a closed wooden door partway down the length of the solid stone wall to my right. *Of course!* I realized. The cellar of the building had to be larger than just this conglomeration of cells. There was probably a laundry area behind that closed door, like the one in my own building building. Ours contained a series of wash tubs, large tables, shelves of hard yellow soap and racks with hangers.

I hurried to the door, took a deep breath and tried the handle. It yielded easily.

I was right.

I stepped into a large laundry room. Father had been right in his suspicions too. The missing people from the list, and they were indeed children as the woman in the courtyard had said, were in here.

Huddled in one corner beside a washtub were about a dozen boys and girls. The oldest, a girl about my age, stood in front of the frightened group, her legs spread and arms crossed across her chest, her dark eyes glaring at me with fierce defiance. A few toys, bundles of clothing, a half-eaten loaf of bread and some other food items lay scattered around them.

"Leave us alone!" the girl commanded. "These are only children. They are not a threat to you!" Clearly, she thought I was there to arrest them and would not let that happen without putting up a fight. Though her courage was impressive, it was also a problem.

"I'm here to help you," I said, knowing how absurd that statement would appear to her, given the uniform I was wearing. "Yes, I was sent to arrest you," I hurried on, "but I have no intention of doing that. Please believe me. I want to help you escape to the back alley. There should be a mule drawn cart there filled with barrels of soup and driven by a Franciscan monk who will take you to a safe place. Please, you must believe me," I begged again, praying silently that indeed Brother Ferenc's wagon would be in the alley by now. If not, what would become of these children once they left here? I refused to dwell on that possibility.

"There isn't much time." I pushed on. "The SS or Arrow Cross will be coming any minute to make sure that I'm carrying out my job properly."

"But you're one of them," the girl said. I could tell by the slight shift of her expression and the softening of her voice that she was leaning towards believing me. That she wanted to believe me. She must have realized that they didn't have many options.

"My gun isn't even loaded," I said, taking advantage of the small inroad I had gained. To carry out my plan, I needed this girl's full trust and cooperation. "See?" I aimed the rifle towards the ceiling and pulled the trigger. We could all clearly hear the click of the empty barrel.

"You must hurry and leave," I insisted. "You can use that back door. There's probably a stairway on the other side that will lead you out to the alley." I pointed to the door that I had noticed at the far end of the room. It was partially concealed by a wooden shelf that had a few cloths and cleaning supplies on it. I barely finished speaking when we heard the creak of the heavy door at the top of the stairs leading to the cellar.

"Quick!" I hissed, "They're coming!" I hoped that the soldiers would be more cautious and slower in their descent than I had been.

As the girl turned to do as I said, I realized that I had to give both her and the other children as much time as possible, even once they all made it through the door, to get away. I had to stall the soldiers so that Brother Ferenc would be able to hide them on his cart. Plus, I had to protect myself. I couldn't be suspected of letting them get away.

"Wait," I said grabbing a hold of the girl's arm. "Take the gun. I know it's not loaded but only my father knows that. If you need to use it, it may deter the guards while you let the children get away." She nodded, but I couldn't let her go just yet. "And before you go, I need you to do something for me too," I added. "To help those soldiers believe the lie that I will tell them and to give yourselves a few extra minutes to get away.

"What?" she asked. "What do you want me to do?"

"Punch me! Knock me out if possible. So that I can tell them that you were bigger and stronger than me. That you overpowered me before I could do anything." The girl looked shocked at my request. She shook her head.

"I can't," she said.

"Yes you can! Use that if you like," I pointed to a loose brick on the floor by one of the laundry tubs. "Or the butt end of the rifle. Maybe draw some blood so it looks more real. I can fake the rest."

"No. You don't understand," she said. "You're saving our lives! I can't hurt you. Not when you're helping us."

I heard the heavy tread of boots descending the stairs. She had to get going!

"You bloody Jew! You vermin!" I hissed at her, trying to remember Father's words. I threw my gun at her as if I intended to knock her off her feet. But, as I suspected, she caught it deftly with one hand. "I should never have offered to help you. I hope you all rot in hell. Every last one of you, you sniveling pigs. You're just a cowardly, stupid girl!"

I searched my brain for more expletives but at that moment the girl's fist connected with the side of my head knocking me back against the wall. Even as I rejoiced that my tactic had worked, I was surprised at the strength of her punch. The back of my head hit hard against the uneven stone surface. Immediately a second punch followed, this time connecting with my nose. I heard a dull thud before my head exploded with pain and everything went dark.

Chapter 33

"Ivan! Ivan! Are you all right? What happened?" The gruff voice seemed to be coming from far away, but the gentle slapping of my face that accompanied it was quite immediate. My whole body trembled and I opened my eyes.

"Thank goodness you're alright! What happened?" It took me a few seconds to realize that I was looking up at Sergeant Farkas, one of Father's men. Two other officers stood behind him, peering over his shoulders.

"I, I don't know," I answered truthfully. For those first few moments my mind was a blank. Then everything that happened came rushing back. I remembered the girl, the children the sound of the footsteps on the stairs. I looked around the room but saw that I was alone in the room with the officers.

How long had I been unconscious? Had the girl and the children all managed to escape? Or had they been arrested and already carted off somewhere? If they did escape, were Brother Ferenc and Tibor there, waiting in the alley with their cart when they emerged from the building?

"Try to remember what happened," Sergeant Farkas urged as he handed me a handkerchief to mop up the blood and quench its flow from my nose. "There must have been someone in here who hit you." I had to suppress a smile as I recalled the strength of the girl's punch. She didn't even need to use a brick to flatten me. "And," Sergeant Farkas added, noticing the toys, "there must have been children here too."

"Yes," I said slowly, drawing out the word. "Yes, there were children." I looked slowly around the empty room, trying to still the dizziness in my head. "Where are they?"

"I don't know" Sergeant Farkas said, clearly puzzled. "We didn't encounter anyone on our way down. Maybe there's another room down here where they're hiding. Go back and search the rest of the cellar!" he ordered one of the guards. "We came straight in here when we saw the light through the open door," he said turning back to me.

"Yes, there, - there was an older boy," I lied. Even in this half-dazed state, I was reluctant to admit that I had been so thoroughly knocked out by a girl. "He was bigger than me. He must have punched me. My rifle's gone."

"Your rifle?"

"Yes," I said. "Father gave it to me, but it wasn't loaded. The boy wouldn't have known that though." The other remaining officer started searching methodically around the laundry tubs and tables. It only took him another minute to notice the exit into the alley.

I held my breath as he pressed down on the handle and pushed the door outwards. It wouldn't budge. He lunged against it and finally the door gave way. In the ray of bright light that streamed into the cellar I noticed a large wooden beam lying cracked in half across the opening. The girl must have placed it there to buy themselves extra time. Again, I repressed a smile. She was as clever as she was strong.

The officer hurried out and I saw his shadow move up the stone steps to street level. Almost immediately he came back inside scowling.

"Nothing," he said. "The alley seems to be deserted."

"Leave them to it," Sergeant Farkas shrugged. "We have other business to attend to. If the children went out there, they will be found. Our men are crawling all over this neighbourhood. Let's get back upstairs and get on with our job." Then he turned to me. "How are you feeling now?" he asked. "Do you think you can get up and come with us?"

"Yes," I nodded and stood up eager to find out if any unplanned arrests had been reported by soldiers in the surrounding streets. The sudden movement made the room spin around me and I reached out my hand to steady myself against the wall. My nose and the area around it throbbed with pain, though the bleeding appeared to have stopped. Sergeant Farkas looked at me with concern.

"Take your time," he said, "My men and I will go on up ahead. I will tell your father what happened and that you'll be all right. When you come back up, take a rest in your father's jeep if you need to, until you feel ready to join us again." With that, he and his men left.

Though I was anxious to know what was going on, I was also relieved to be on my own again. I waited till all the footsteps had died away and then cautiously made my way over to the back door. I opened it and peered up and down the alley, but as the guard had said, there were no signs of life. I sighed, wondering if the plan had worked. Or had Brother Ferenc, Tibor and the children all been caught and arrested?

The courtyard was deserted by the time I made my way up the stairs. Out on the street I saw that the group of prisoners had grown and had been marched farther down to the next building marked with a yellow star. Ignoring Sergeant Farkas's advice to rest, I walked over and tried to catch snatches of conversation between the guards. Though some spoke in German so I only understood a few words, I was certain that there was no mention of a wagon full of escaped children. I didn't recognize any of the faces from the cellar among the throng of frightened people huddled together. Certainly not the girl who had punched me.

I hung about in the street until the newest prisoners were marched out of the building to join the group. I was glad that I now had an excuse to not participate in the arrests. I doubted that I would have another opportunity like the one I just had to rescue anyone. After one more building the quota for the day had been reached and the assembled Jews were marched towards the train station. Father, together with Zoltan and his father, hurried over when he saw me. They all wanted to hear again from me, what had happened. Though I had failed at my assigned task, because of my injuries I had momentarily gained hero status. Even Zoltan examined my bruised face with admiration. Perhaps now he would lay off taunting me, I hoped.

To my relief, there was no talk of hunting for any escaped children who might be hidden in the alleyways.

As the group of prisoners shuffled past us, I noticed the woman who had spoken up in the courtyard. Like the others, her shoulders were hunched and her eyes were filled with fear. Yet, around her mouth I detected a slight smile of satisfaction. Not everything had turned out as the enemy had planned.

Chapter 34

When I heard a knock on our front door early the next afternoon, just as we were finishing our Sunday dinner, my heart skipped a beat. It was the time when Jakob and I used to take off for our adventures and for an instant I thought it was him. But then I realized that of course that could not be. Still, I hurried to open the door and though it was Tibor and not Jakob standing there, I was happily surprised.

"Wow, that's a wicked bruise," Tibor whistled as soon as he saw my face. "Will it stop you from coming outside?" he asked, holding out a soccer ball. I suspected that the soccer ball was just the excuse. He had come to tell me his side of the previous day and I was eager to hear it. Mother and Father used to be happy to see me take off with Jakob on Sunday afternoons. It allowed them some time alone in which to talk and relax. I figured that leaving with Tibor wouldn't be an issue. Yet, when Father came up behind me, I could hear the frown in his voice even before I turned around and looked up at him.

"What is this?" he asked, "Aren't you the son of that reporter, Adam Pap? He's always around snapping pictures and getting in the way when we're busy, trying to do our job."

"Yes sir!" Tibor said proudly, ignoring Father's scowl. "My father writes articles and takes pictures for the Harc newspaper." Tibor reached out his hand to shake Father's. I saw Father hesitate for an instant before he grasped Tibor's hand in return.

"Yes. Well," Father said, sounding confused, "what are you doing here? What do you want with Ivan?"

"To play soccer sir," Tibor replied. "Just over in the park down the street. I thought it might be fun."

"Yes. Well," Father repeated gruffly, thrown off balance by Tibor's show of confidence. "You can see Ivan is in no condition to be playing soccer."

"Please Father," I begged. "My feet aren't bothered by the bruise on my face. I'm feeling perfectly fine now. And I'll be careful. I promise."

"We won't be rough sir," Tibor added. "I will take full responsibility for Ivan's well-being." This time, Father was clearly trying to suppress a smile.

"Very well," he agreed. "Make sure you don't stay out too long," he said turning to me. "And do be careful!"

"I'll be back within a couple of hours," I assured him.

Tibor and I turned and ran off before he had a chance to reconsider.

"Come on!" Tibor shouted once we were out in the street. He kicked the soccer ball into the next window well than grabbed my arm. "I'll take you to them." He added with a wide smile across his face.

"To them?" I asked, barely daring to hope at what he meant. He nodded as we hurried along.

"The children that we saved," he said, lowering his voice. Not that there was much need. The street, in the middle of this cool Sunday afternoon, was mostly deserted and looked peaceful. The only other sounds came from the bare branches of the chestnuts rustling in the breeze and the crunch of brown leaves beneath our feet.

"So you got them?" I asked, slowing our pace. "They're safe?" Again, Tibor nodded.

"It worked just as we planned," he said. "But it's a good thing that you got knocked out. We assumed that the guards' concern over you delayed them from coming out into the alley sooner. Judit told us about how you goaded her into punching you. She feels horrible about it now, though she understands why you did it.

"At any rate, we managed to get everyone loaded onto the cart and spread the tarp over them, then moved on, out of the alley. We crossed the street into another alley, heading in the general direction of Mr. Wallenberg's safe house."

Tibor paused for a moment as he hopped onto a passing number 6 streetcar and pulled me after him as it slowly clanked along its tracks. I assumed we were headed to the safe house. We remained outside, swaying on the landing platform where we had more privacy and where hopefully, we could avoid having to show tickets that we didn't have.

"About ten minutes after we left," Tibor continued, "we were stopped by two SS soldiers.

They ordered Brother Ferenc to get down and show them the barrels of soup. Thank goodness Brother Ferenc had judged right. After they saw the first couple of barrels at the back end of the cart full of soup, they were satisfied and didn't waste any more time with us." Tibor took a deep breath and shook his head. "But it was tense, I tell you. I was sweating up in the front seat despite the coldness of the day."

"Brother Ferenc told the soldiers that we were taking the back alleyways as much as possible in order to avoid the commotion in the streets with all the prisoners being rounded up," Tibor continued, "which of course was true as well. At any rate, there was no way we could risk turning up behind Korona Street again that day. If you had sent any more people out, they would have been left to fend for themselves. Though after hearing Judit's account, we doubted that you were in any condition to do much more rescuing."

"Judit?" I asked, though I knew immediately who she must be.

"Yes, Judit," Tibor chuckled. "That's the name of the girl in charge of the younger children, she was very upset once she realized that they were safe and everything had been planned by us to save them.

'I can't believe I punched him so hard'," Tibor mimicked her voice. "She kept saying it over and over again, covering her face with her hands. She said that you said some nasty things to her to make her angry. She said it worked. She said she just couldn't help it. Her fist just flew at you. She refused to repeat any of what you said." He looked at me expectantly. When I remained silent, he poked me in the ribs. "Come on, what did you say to her?" he asked.

"I don't remember exactly," I shrugged, embarrassed by the things I had said. "I just repeated some stuff I had heard Father say about the Jews. I needed her to punch me so that I could tell the guards that I was overpowered. But later, when I came to, I told them it was by a boy," I admitted, flushing. "I never dreamt that she would be that strong. I just needed a bruise and a bit of blood. I thought I would have to fake the unconscious bit."

"Yes," Tibor nodded and chuckled. "She seems pretty tough for a girl. And surprisingly strong, given how small she is. I don't think she'll sleep again tonight if she can't see you and tell you face to face how sorry she is for what she did to you." Tibor glanced at me out of the corner of his eye. "That's why I've been commissioned so urgently to see how you are and to get you to come with me if at all possible."

"Oh." I said simply, at a loss for words.

"Hey, this is our stop!" Tibor yelled suddenly, and we both made a leap to the concrete platform of the station.

I followed Tibor without paying attention to the area we passed through. I was too preoccupied with my upcoming encounter with Judit.

Chapter 35

Tho building wo walkod up to, was just like all the others on the street. It was a squat, four story, yellow brick cube with a flat façade. The only adornment on the outside was a plaque beside the front gate displaying the Swedish emblem and declaring the building to be a property of the Swedish Government.

The large, double entrance doors were locked, and Tibor tugged on a chord that hung from a small, metal box on the right-hand side. A loud bell reverberated on the other side. We waited almost two minutes before a deep male voice asked what we wanted.

"It's Tibor Pap here, to see the Varga family with my friend Ivan."

I was shocked to hear him say that we were here to see the Vargas. What were they doing here? And how did Tibor know about them? How much did he know? I didn't recall having said anything to Tibor about the circumstances of their disappearance.

Immediately we heard the lifting of a heavy metal bar and the door swung open a crack.

"Good to see you again so soon, Mr. Pap," said the elderly man who opened the door for us said as we slipped inside. "You know your way, I assume."

"Yes sir," Tibor said as the heavy door slammed shut behind us and the man turned to lock it again. We stepped into a small, stone tiled foyer. Traditional balconies on each floor skirted the courtyard to the left and right, visible through a frosted glass doorway. Most of the doors opening onto the courtyard were open and people milled about on the balconies and the cobbled stone surface of the courtyard.

"It's getting pretty crowded in some of those apartments, thanks to Mr. Wallenberg's efforts," Tibor explained. "But the people in here don't complain about the conditions. They know they are the lucky ones and are more focused on helping each other out. Come, our friends are up on the third floor."

"Wait!" I said, laying a restraining hand on Tibor's shoulder. "You said that we're here to see the Vargas. They're here?"

"Yes. Sorry. In all the excitement I forgot to mention that Brother Ferenc, together with Mr. Wallenberg of course, arranged for their transfer here on Friday evening." Tibor turned and opened the glass doors that led to a wide, stone stairwell. I followed close behind not wanting to miss a word of what he said. "They are safe here. Neither the Arrow Cross nor the Nazis have authority to enter a building that is under Swedish protection. For now, the Nazis are ensuring that everyone respects those rules. I met the Vargas and their housekeeper as well as Aunt Mimi and Lilly when we brought the children here on Saturday."

We mounted the stairs two at a time as Tibor talked. We wove among the groups of chattering people on the third-floor balcony till we arrived at the corner apartment. Though this door too was ajar, Tibor knocked politely and we waited till Mrs. Varga appeared.

"Ivan, Tibor," she exclaimed, "come in, come in. We are all so proud of what you have done. Oh, look at your face, Ivan," she said gently brushing a finger against my cheek, "I hope it doesn't hurt too much. You were so brave! We are all so proud of you!" she repeated. I was quite embarrassed by her profuse welcome.

"I'm surprised to see you here," I said, wanting to divert the attention away from myself.

"Yes. We couldn't really stay at the embassy for much longer," she explained. "It's not intended to house people like us. And we came here just in time. The children you rescued needed someone to look after them and Mr. Wallenberg asked if we would like to take on that responsibility. Of course we said yes. It's the least we can do to help. Besides, it's good for us to have something to take our minds off our own troubles. At least we adults understand what is happening in the world, but these children..." her voice trailed off as she glanced behind her at the bustling room.

I noticed Lilly sitting on a worn couch with a bunch of toddlers squeezed in next to her, her arm wrapped around a curly haired little girl, while with the other she held open a large picture book. Lilly looked very different from the pale frightened girl I had seen a few days ago. Her cheeks were flushed, her eyes sparkled and her voice, as she read out loud, sounded lighthearted and happy.

"Yes," Mrs. Varga said, following my gaze. "This has been good for all of us, but especially for Lilly and my sister. The recent events have been so much harder on them. At least," her voice broke and for an uncomfortable moment I feared that she was going to dissolve into tears. But then she took a deep breath and regained her self-control. "At least I still have hope. Hope that I will see my Jakob again.

"But come, come on in and meet everyone."

She ushered us into the room and as I looked around at the busy collection of children and adults, one body disengaged itself from a group huddled around a board game on the floor. She stood up straight and walked towards me. It was Judit, the girl in charge in the cellar.

"Hello Ivan," she said, then turned towards Tibor. "And thank *you* for bringing him." Without waiting for a response, she turned back to me and continued. "I want to thank you for saving our lives yesterday," she said. "And I'm sorry that I doubted your intentions at first and that I punched you so hard." Here she smiled involuntarily, and her eyes twinkled for a moment before her expression grew serious again.

"I know you only wanted to *appear* hurt so that you had an explanation for the SS and Arrow Cross, but – but the things you said," she faltered, "well, they just made me so angry. I couldn't help it. My fist just seemed to fly out on its own accord. I'm sorry," she looked down, suddenly appearing ill at ease. "I should have just done as you asked right away." She took a deep breath, as if relieved that this part of our encounter was over. Her smile returned. She reached out and took my hand in one of hers and Tibor's in the other.

"Come," she said, pulling us forward, "I'll introduce you to the children. I hope they won't be frightened by your bruise. It's turning a rather interesting shade of purple."

She led us around the apartment, which was composed of a large living room, a spacious kitchen containing a round table surrounded by several chairs, two bedrooms and a bathroom. Though it would have served one family well, with the three adults, two teenage girls and about twenty younger children, it was crowded. Sleeping mats and bedding were rolled up against the walls of the bedrooms. The children seemed relatively contented and occupied, drawing or playing simple makeshift games. Most important, they were alive and had a safe place to stay. They were the lucky ones. For a moment I allowed myself a sigh of satisfaction at the role I had played in bringing this about. Though I wished that I could have done more, this was fine for now.

Our stay was brief. I had promised Father that I would be back within a couple of hours and I didn't want to disappoint him on that account. With all the detours due to bombed out roads and scattered rubble from buildings, getting around the city was a lengthy business. Much as I longed to stay, after a brief visit with the Vargas in which I told them that I had no further news of Jakob, I was anxious to leave.

Judit followed us to the door. As I placed my hand on the door handle, she grabbed hold of my arm.

"Ivan," she said, looking at me with an intensity that made my knees feel suddenly weak, "I want to help. I want to do what you do. Rescue people. Help others in any way I can. It's why I volunteered to take charge of the children in our building. At the time it was the only way I could be of use. Please, let me come along the next time."

I was taken aback by this unexpected request. Hadn't she been through enough already?

"I, I don't know," I stammered. "I don't know if I will be able to do any actual rescuing again. My only task is to inform Mr. Wallenberg of where the Nazis and Arrow Cross are going to arrest people. The rescue yesterday just happened to work out. My father is an Arrow Cross commander. I can't risk him finding out what I'm doing. And if he discovers where the Vargas are, he could have them all killed. I have to be very careful."

"I know," she nodded. "But I can't just sit around and do nothing, saving my own skin while others suffer." Her voice grew vehement. "My mother – she was among those marched out of the building yesterday. My father was taken months ago, and we haven't heard from him since. I won't stand by and keep letting that happen to others. If I can't help *your* efforts, I will have to find another way."

"All right," I said in a rush, suddenly worried that she might bolt from the safety of the apartment that very instant. Why couldn't she be content with just being safe, like Lilly was? "I'll see what I can do. But it's not up to me of course. It's Mr. Wallenberg who makes all the decisions about what is to be done."

"I've heard enough about you that I know you can think and act for yourself," she said. "I'm counting on that." Then she turned and went back into the room.

Chapter 36

My discoloured and swollen face gained me a special status at school on Monday. People looked at me with an air of awe and respect. Zoltan, as I had hoped, remained in the background and said little. I was grateful that no one besides Tibor knew that the person who had inflicted those impressive bruises was a girl. By now, I knew that I could count on Tibor's loyalty one hundred per cent.

Within a few days, my bruise faded, and life seemed to go back to its normal routine. As normal that is, as it could be in the midst of war.

I managed to pass information to Mr. Wallenberg a few more times through Brother Ferenc about the specific locations of planned Jewish arrests. Once, I even snuck into Father's office and hastily copied down a few names from one of the documents on Father's desk. But with the increased fighting, Father was home less and less. Often, he wouldn't return till I was in bed asleep. In the morning, if he was still at home, he was too preoccupied with the upcoming day to say more than a brief 'good morning'. Sometimes he spent entire nights at his office, catching a few hours of sleep while sitting in his chair.

Each day of November the fighting in and around Budapest intensified. The local newspapers and radio stations only reported the heroic efforts of the Nazis and Arrow Cross to ward off the advancing Russian troops. But through his father, Tibor learned that the Allied forces were steadily getting closer to the city. Even our own neighbourhood was no longer a safe haven.

"Ivan, wake up! We must hurry! Wake up!" I slowly emerged from the foggy realm of sleep and looked up into Mother's agitated face. She was vehemently shaking my shoulders.

"What? What is it?" I asked rubbing my eyes. I barely finished my question when the entire building around me trembled. I heard the not so distant sound of an explosion.

"Please, we have to hurry and get to the bomb shelter! It's not safe here!" There was another tremble. Another explosion. Closer this time.

I jumped out of bed and looked out the window. My bedroom window faced out into the roofless courtyard. An eerie orange light lit up the night sky. Flares! I knew that these slowly descending torches were dropped by allied planes, our supposed enemies, to shed light on their intended targets. They would be followed by bombs. The problem was that the planes often missed and hit residential areas and apartment buildings, destroying homes and killing people.

Until recently most of the fighting had been over on the Pest side of the Danube. But now it was everywhere. All around us.

"It's because of the Citadel on Gellert Mountain and the German battalion stationed there," Father had warned us a couple of weeks ago. "It will be one of the prime targets of the Russians and Americans." I could see at the time how much it pained Father to admit our vulnerability. While secretly elated that the Allies were making progress, I also felt sorry for Father. And I was frightened. Would we survive all this fighting? Were the Vargas and others in the 'Safe' houses still safe?

"If that happens, you must get down to the bomb shelter at once," Father had insisted. Mother and I nodded silently and with his help we prepared an emergency rations package to take with us.

The time for it had come. We hurried down to the cellar where just a few weeks ago I had led the Vargas to the hidden passage. If our building was over bombed, I might have to lead Mother and the others gathered here out that way to safety.

We were one of the last ones to arrive in the basement, dimly lit by a few oil lamps. Groups of people from our building were huddled in the cells where they had spread blankets next to the meagre piles of coal. Fuel, like everything else, was in short supply this winter so there was plenty of space.

A hush fell over the room as we entered. The muffled chatter that had been audible from the hallway suddenly died away. All eyes looked at us suspiciously. Though Father wasn't with us on account of his work, everyone in the building knew that he was an Arrow Cross commander. Everyone feared him. We, as his family, could be his informants. One wrong word could easily get a person sent to prison or the camps. At one time I would have been proud of Father's power. Now, understanding more fully the kind of power he wielded, it only brought me shame.

"Would you like some biscuits?" Mother reached a small tin towards our neighbor in the adjoining cell after we had settled down on our own blanket. Slowly, by sharing our food and reassuring people with small talk, she managed to erase the tension in the cellar. The anxious chatter returned, children started to run around and play hide and go seek. It was only when the building above us shook and we both heard and felt the force of a nearby explosion that sudden silence descended again as everyone held their breath till the danger had passed.

We had been in the cellar for several hours before the wail of the siren sounded announcing that it was safe to return above ground. To our relief our building, as well as most of our neighbourhood had survived. The bombing was not quite as close as it had felt. Still, after that, whenever we heard the siren announcing an air raid and saw the flairs light up the skies, we hurried below ground. Often this happened several nights a week. Mattresses and cots were moved down to the cellar from other bombed or abandoned apartments. The cellar became our second home.

Chapter 37

Sat., Dec.9

To my relief Father was too busy now to take me with him again on Saturdays. After putting in the required training hours with the Levente group in the morning, the rest of my Saturday was free. I decided to take the few, small items I had saved from their home, to the Vargas. I had put off going to see them, not only because it was difficult to sneak over there undetected, but because I still hadn't thought of a way to involve Judit in rescuing or hiding Jews. I was reluctant to see her disappointment in me.

I was just about to leave my building, when Tibor rushed in, almost colliding with me. I could tell at a glance that something was very wrong.

"Ivan," he said, grabbing my arm, "you have to help me. I don't know what to do. My father was arrested this morning by some Arrow Cross soldiers. They accused him of spying and sending photographs to their enemies. They said he was a traitor and he was going to be punished. Please, can you please talk to your father at once? See if he can stop them? I can't think of anyone else who could help. Not even Mr. Wallenberg."

Tibor's words sent a chill through me.

"We've stopped wasting our time with having traitors against our country tried by tribunals," Father had said a few days earlier. *"It's one area where the Nazis don't dictate what we do. I sent three men who were arrested this morning to join the execution line of Jews this afternoon. Now that's being efficient,"* he had concluded with a pleased look. Father had been right in his earlier prediction. Besides being transported to the camps, Jews were now also being lined up daily along the banks of the Danube and shot into the river. Tibor's father would probably be forced to join them.

"Alright," I said, abandoning my plan to visit the Vargas, "I'll put this box back in my room and then we'll go to Father's office at once. Wait here."

Within minutes, Tibor and I were racing to the Arrow Cross headquarters on the Pest side of the river. We alternated between running and hopping on and off streetcars and busses. Several of the transportation lines were detoured or closed because of the piles of rubble everywhere. We cut across those on foot.

At last we reached the four-story building on the corner of Andrassy and Csengery Streets. I had been here before with Father, but this was the first time that I thought about what the nickname for this building, 'House of Terror' might actually imply.

The small basement windows just above ground level were made of opaque frosted glass, heavily fortified with black metal grills. Father had told me previously that those were mostly holding cells for prisoners. Some were maybe even rooms of torture. Was Tibor's father in one of them now?

"Let me do the talking," I said as I pushed open the heavy wooden door. To my relief, the guard inside recognized me.

"Your father is in his office," he said without questioning our presence there. "His secretary will let you know if he is free to see you."

"Thank you," I said and hurried down the wide foyer to the marble stairway, with Tibor following at my side. We ran up the stairs two at a time to the third floor where Father's office was located. The door to his reception area stood open and his secretary, Private Janos, was sitting at a wooden desk. On it was a large black typewriter and an array of documents and charts.

"Ivan," Private Janos said and stood upon seeing me. "It's a surprise to see you here. Is everything all right at home with your mother?" He came around the desk and shook my hand.

"Yes," I said. "Everything's fine at home. But my friend Tibor and I need to see Father right away. It's very urgent." Private Janos glanced at Tibor but did not offer to shake his hand.

"I will see what I can do," he said turning towards the door that led to Father's office. He knocked lightly, then without waiting for a reply, he entered, pulling the door shut behind him.

Tibor and I stood in silence, straining to catch the meaning of the muffled sounds behind the door. In a couple of minutes it opened and Private Janos stepped out leaving it wide open behind him.

"Sergeant Biro will see you and your friend now," he said with a curt nod. Tibor and I went in. Father and another man whom I did not recognize stood behind a long table examining a large colourful map spread on its surface.

"Ivan, what brings you here?" Father asked looking up from the map with a frown. "If everything is fine at home, what can be so urgent? You know how busy I am."

"Yes Father," I said stepping towards the table. "I'm sorry to bother you but this *is* very urgent." Father, guessing that we wanted to speak to him privately when I didn't say anything else, glanced at the man by his side.

"Please excuse us for a minute. I'm sure this won't take long," he said. The man nodded and left the room, closing the door behind him.

"This is my friend Tibor," I said as soon as the three of us were alone. "He came to the house a few weeks ago after I was injured."

"Yes, Yes." Father said with an air of impatience. "I remember him. He is in your class at school. His father is that photographer. The two of you went to play soccer."

"Yes," I nodded, suppressing a pang of guilt as I recalled how we had deceived Father that day. "Well, this morning Tibor's father was arrested by some Arrow Cross soldiers. They said he was going to be shot. I, we," I said looking towards Tibor, "we were wondering if you could stop them. Please," I added.

"Ah," said Father his frown deepening. "So that's the man they arrested. Adam Papp. I don't think they mentioned his name when I was told of the arrest." A flush of red crept up Father's neck and face, a common warning sign of his mounting anger. "Adam Papp," he repeated.

"Yes. I have had my suspicions about him for quite some time now," Father said looking directly at Tibor. "He has been taking too many unnecessary pictures! He has been writing articles that are not true!" Father's voice rose with each sentence. "We discovered that he has taken several photographs and presented them out of context, trying to undermine the work we are doing. He has sent these articles to our enemies.

"I'm sorry," Father shook his head, "but your father has been a traitor to our cause. Be very careful" he continued, his voice almost dropping to a whisper. He jabbed his finger at Tibor's chest. "I could have you arrested as well! And how dare you involve Ivan, my son, in this?"

"Please sir," Tibor said, his voice trembling. "I'm sorry if my father did something he shouldn't have. Maybe he didn't know that it was wrong. I'm sure he regrets doing anything against the regime. Please sir," Tibor repeated, "he is my father. Can you please at least stop them from killing him?"

I knew that Tibor was not sorry for what his father had done. In fact, he must be very proud of him. I thought of those cells in the basement of this 'House of Terror'. It would be horrible to be imprisoned there. But it was better than being killed.

"Please Father," I said taking a step forward so that I was within arm's reach of him. "If it was you who got arrested and were in danger of being killed, I too would do the same for you. I would beg whoever was in charge to spare your life, no matter what the risk was to me, because I love you. If Tibor's father truly did something wrong, couldn't he just be punished? I don't want to lose another friend. Please, don't let them kill Tibor's father."

Father opened his mouth to say something, then closed it again without saying a word. He looked down at his desk as if contemplating some small section of the map. Tibor and I held our breaths, waiting.

"It might be too late," Father said at last, looking up, first at me, then settling his gaze on Tibor. "After his arrest, your father was brought here to be questioned. Then, a short while ago, he was taken down to the Danube to stand with the Jews scheduled to be executed there today.

"I will not hold you accountable for your father's actions. After all, you are a young man now, like Ivan, capable of making your own choices. I will let you go in the hopes that through your friendship with my son, you will make better choices than your father did. But I cannot excuse your father's duplicity. For this he must be punished.

"But," Father said loudly and held up his hand to stop Tibor from uttering any words of protest. "I will not have him killed. I will spare his life for now. He can join the prisoners marching out of the city to Auschwitz. We shall see how he fares with that. He might end up regretting that he was not executed today." Father grabbed a sheet of paper from his desk and scribbled something on it. He walked brusquely to the door and handed it to the officer waiting on the other side.

"Go! Take this immediately to the Captain at the ramparts and demand that Adam Papp be pulled from the firing line. He will be going to Auschwitz instead. Hurry!" Father added as the man turned to leave, "before it is too late!"

Chapter 38

Auschwitz! I chill ran down my spine. From what I had learned about the concentration camp, I wondered, as Father implied, if it was indeed worse than a quick death. Tibor, however, seemed relieved.

"Thank you, sir," he said to Father as soon as the man left. "My father is a strong man. I have hope now that I will see him again."

"We shall see," said Father, his voice grim, his brows once again creased into a frown. "I must get back to work now." He turned his attention to the map on the table. I noticed there were several red X's on it and blue lines with arrows at the end flaring out from the Buda side of the city. I wondered what it all meant but didn't ask. It was clear that Father expected us to leave immediately. With a hastily mumbled goodbye, we took our leave.

"Come," Tibor grabbed my arm as soon as the door closed behind us, "maybe we can get to the river in time to see my father before he is taken away. I want to make sure your father's man is not too late." Ignoring Private Janos calling after us, we leapt down the stairs and bounded out the front door. Deciding that taking the subway might be our quickest way to reach the Danube, we ran to the station below Andrassy St., jumped over the gate and hopped onto the train just before the doors closed and it pulled away.

Tense with suspense at what we would find when we reached the ramparts bordering the river, we rode in silence. We had spent barely ten minutes in Father's office, but those ten minutes could make the difference between life and death.

I thought back to Father's words to Tibor back in his office. What he had said about Tibor making his own choices. He was repeating what Brother Ferenc had said to our class at the beginning of the school year. Would Father be as understanding if he knew that the choices I made differed from his? I knew that I was not yet prepared to find out.

Underground, there were no piles of rubble obstructing our way and we arrived at the ramparts in less than fifteen minutes. We dismounted from the subway car, leapt up the stairs two at a time and emerged at the foot of the Chain Bridge.

To the left of the bridge, as we faced the river, everything looked relatively normal. Lorries and cars moved slowly along the road. Large barges were tied up to the black bollards that dotted the rampart walls. Civilians with their heads down, as if not wanting to witness what was happening upstream, hurried along.

To our right we saw a disheveled line of men, women and children lined up in a long solitary row on the low, flat wall of the rampart facing the river. Behind them stood Arrow Cross soldiers, their guns, for the time being, lowered at their sides. Farther back, more prisoners were held under guard. We hurried in their direction but had to stop after a few steps as a group of SS soldiers blocked our path. We scrambled onto a nearby bench to get a better view. I squeezed my eyes shut, not wanting to believe what I was seeing. I had known this was happening now daily, but I had never been this close to the actual execution line. All those people were destined to die. Would Father's messenger arrive in time to have Tibor's father pulled from amongst them?

I felt a tug on my sleeve.

"Over there. Look!" Tibor said, pointing to the far end of the line of prisoners. I did as he said and immediately recognized the distinct figure of Raul Wallenberg. His long overcoat was open, his scarf askew. I also recognized his aide at his side, holding a small stack of documents. A few prisoners must have already been pulled from the line for they were huddled nearby, identifiable as Jews by the bright yellow star on their garments. I wondered if any of the information I had supplied during the past week had helped to save some of these lives.

"Can you see your father?" I asked Tibor. He shook his head.

"It's too difficult to tell from here," he said. "They all have their backs to us. We have to get closer."

"No!" I grabbed a hold of Tibor's jacket before he had a chance to jump off the bench. "There's no point in trying. The guards won't let you get close or they'll arrest you if you try to push past. We're best off up here."

Just as I finished speaking, a man approached from the road behind us and spoke to one of the SS officers. He was Father's man! He probably had to make several detours before he could reach this spot in an army vehicle. Tibor and I had made quicker progress on the subway.

Tibor recognized him as well. He gripped my arm and we watched in silence as the man was led to the commander in charge of the firing squad. Together they walked down the line of prisoners, questioning each one. We could hear nothing of what was being said from our location.

They were nearing the end of the row when one of the prisoners turned his head and stepped out of line.

"It's Father!" gasped Tibor gripping my arm tighter. "He's wearing the green sweater that Mother knit for him last Christmas. And that's definitely his cap!" There was a brief exchange between the men and Tibor's father was led away with his arms tied behind his back.

"Come!" Tibor jumped down from the bench, and ran along the ramparts in their direction, on the street, rather than the river side, behind the SS guards and the other prisoners. I rushed after him. No one stood in our way.

We caught up to them as they crossed the road and turned right stopping next to a parked army Jeep.

"Father!" Tibor called out. The guard did not hear as he was busy fumbling with the keys. But Tibor's father turned his head in our direction. His face lit up with a sad smile as he recognized Tibor. He gave a short nod before he was roughly pushed inside the waiting vehicle.

"At least he knows that I know, and that I can tell Mother what has happened to him. And that he is still alive." Tibor let out a long sigh. "It's a small comfort, but it's something. Enough to give us hope."

We watched as the Jeep started up and turned onto the ramparts, passing right in front of us, heading in the direction of the Western Railway Station – the starting point of the long march towards Auschwitz.

Chapter 39

Tibor arrived at school on Monday looking pale and distracted.

"I wanted to stay home with Mother, but she insisted that I come," he explained as we hung up our jackets in the cloak room. The other boys were bustling around ignoring us, but still we kept our voices low. "She said Father would want me to continue to do my best at school. Besides, she said there's nothing to be gained by just sitting around and worrying about Father or what may happen to us next. The safest thing to do is to go about our business as usual. I hope she's right. Though it's hard to put Father out of my mind. I can't imagine what he must be going through."

"I know," I said. "I felt the same way when Hendrik was first taken. I'm always wondering what might be happening with him or even if he's even still alive. Your mother's right. It's good to keep busy. Especially doing things to fight back. Things like helping Judit and the others in the safe houses. I don't know," I shrugged, "but it's as if, through them, you're also helping the person that you can't do anything for. At least it sort of feels like that."

Then I had another thought. "How will you manage without your father's income?" I asked. I knew that getting sufficient food and other supplies was a constant concern for most people these days. Almost as worrisome as safety.

"Mother's a seamstress," Tibor said. "Even now with the war, she has some mending and tailoring jobs. Hopefully that will help us get by. Plus, a couple of mysterious packages have been left outside our front door since Father's arrest." Tibor smiled and for a moment the lines of worry dissolved from around his eyes and mouth. "Someone left a loaf of bread on Sunday. This morning I nearly stepped on a large chunk of sausage wrapped in paper. We even got an envelope with a small amount of cash. No names were left with anything. Everyone is too scared to be discovered helping the family of an alleged traitor. But it's good to know that we still have friends."

"And enemies unfortunately," I said with a nod towards the cloak room door through which Zoltan had just entered.

"Heard your father was arrested, Papp," he said with a sneer as soon as he saw us. "Feeding information to the enemy. No wonder you're suddenly such close friends with the school's traitor." A hush fell over the room at Zoltan's words. All eyes turned towards Tibor and me. Tibor's face turned red, but he straightened up and boldly answered back.

"My father's a photo journalist. He was merely doing his job, reporting what he sees. What all of us can see every day if we only care to look. Aren't you proud of what the Arrow Cross and the Nazis are doing? And if you are, why don't you want the whole world to know about it? Or do you secretly think it's wrong? Something to be hidden and ashamed of? Is that why you're happy that my father was arrested? Arresting him was a big mistake on the part of the Arrow Cross and once people in power figure it out, he'll be released."

I was impressed with the twisted logic that Tibor came up with in defense of his father. Unfortunately, Zoltan would have none of it. He wasn't quite as thick headed as he looked.

"Don't hold your breath," he said striding angrily over to us. "You don't know what you're talking about! Of course I'm proud of what we're doing. We *should* be getting rid of the Jews and all those other low bloods like the gypsies, cripples and other weirdos. It's the countries that are fighting us that don't understand that this is the only way to become a strong and powerful and pure nation. That's also why we'll win this war despite traitors like your father. Because we're better than everyone else." Zoltan shoved Tibor back into the coats as he uttered the final words. The other boys surrounding us stepped back and pressed against the walls. A few hurried from the room.

I pushed between Zoltan and Tibor.

"Leave him alone!" I said, trying to remain calm. "It's rather cowardly to be attacking someone so much smaller than you. Why not shove me instead?" I taunted.

Zoltan spat and his saliva hit my left shoulder.

"I wouldn't waste my time or energy on a Jew lover," he said, starting to turn away. Before he completely turned his head, I raised my fist and delivered a satisfying punch to the side of his jaw. A punch that in my opinion more than equaled the one I had received from Judit. Zoltan yelped in pain and his hands flew up to cover his mouth. I saw a small trickle of blood ooze out from between his fingers. I must have loosened a tooth, I guessed, or else he bit his tongue. Either way, I wasn't too concerned. I figured he'd be too embarrassed to go tattle-taling on me.

"Think of that before you go calling either of us names again," I said, noting that this time none of Zoltan's close buddies happened to be around. No one came rushing to his aid. Before he could think of a response, the first bell rang and everyone hurried from the cloak room, eager to leave the confrontation behind them. I pulled a clean handkerchief Mother had given me that morning from my pocket.

"Here, you can use this," I said, tossing it in Zoltan's direction as Tibor and I followed the others. Zoltan reached out with his free hand, the one not clamped over his chin and mouth, and caught the handkerchief in midair. His thanks was a glare full of hatred and the promise of revenge.

Chapter 40

Our math class was interrupted that morning by a trip to the monastery's bomb shelter. This had become a common practice. The air raid sirens warning us of an attack seemed to be going off incessantly, sometimes three or four times a day. In the shelter, the brothers carried on our lessons in hushed voices by the light of a flickering candle, careful not to disturb the other classes huddled with their own instructors in the shadows of the cavernous room. Sometimes, if the fighting didn't appear to be too close, we ignored the sirens and carried on with our lessons above ground. The decision to stay or hide was left up to Abbot Tomas, the head of the monastery.

A similar disregard for danger prevailed throughout the city. Though some neighbourhoods were almost completely in ruins, life in others like ours, carried on.

Then, in mid-December we learned that the Soviet troops had penetrated the Eastern borders of Hungary and were steadily advancing towards Budapest. While I knew that many people secretly hoped that the Russians would drive the Nazi troops from our country, the general attitude expressed openly in school and in the streets was still one of arrogant confidence. The newspaper headlines declared, and radios blared that the joint power of the Nazi and Arrow Cross troops would defeat the advancing Russians.

Thus, it was a shock when we learned on the 26th, right after Christmas Day, that during the night, the Soviet troops had surrounded our city and blocked all the roads and rail lines leading in or out. Budapest was under siege! Mother and I now understood why Father had been unable to join us for Christmas celebrations two nights earlier and why he hadn't had time to come home since.

As usual, Mother and I had decorated the tree on the afternoon of the 24th. It was a smaller tree than we normally had, and I had easily carried it home over the few blocks from the market and up the stairs to our apartment.

"We're fortunate that we can have a tree at all," Mother reminded me when she saw my dismayed look once we cut the rough string and loosened the tree's branches. "Everything is so scarce these days. We'll stand it on this side table and then it will look taller," she said, trying to be cheerful. "And," she added, "I managed to buy one of the last carps at the market so we can still have our traditional fish soup for supper."

I glanced across the courtyard to the windows where Jakob used to live. I thought of the big tree that they used to erect right behind the kitchen window. I had always thought that it was a strange place to put the tree. It was where we had our table on our side. Our tree was in the living room. But now I realized that they had probably wanted to make sure that everyone in the building saw the tree and believed them to be Christians. Another family had already moved into the apartment and if they had a tree, it too was probably in their living room. They had nothing to prove. I wondered where Jakob was right now. Was he able to keep track of the days? Did he know that it was Christmas Eve? Did it still matter to him?

I knew now that instead of Christmas, the Jewish people in the safe houses celebrated a festival called Hannukah which had started several days ago and lasted for eight days in total. The Vargas, Aunt Mimi, Lilly, Judit and Hannah had all tried at once to explain its significance to me the last time I had visited. The main thing I remembered from amongst the many details was the tradition of lighting candles. Well, we had lots of candles on our tree and in my heart, I joined our celebration to theirs.

Mother and I had walked to St. Magdalen's church that evening for the late-night Mass. It felt strange without Father's presence beside us. We hadn't heard from him in days and though she tried to hide it, I knew that Mother was sick with worry about him. She wrapped her arm through mine and leaned into me as we made our way along the icy cobblestone street. For the first time I realized that now I was indeed considerably taller and broader than her. A true 'man of the house' when Father was not there.

The Mass that night did not leave us with the usual peaceful and joyful feeling. Thankfully the sirens were silent and there was no need to hurry to the bomb shelter. Yet, despite the angelic sounds of the choir, despite the warm glow of candles shimmering against the ornate gold trim and stained glass windows of the church and despite the priest's homily that focused on the message of hope through the Saviour's birth, the tension and fear amongst the congregation was palpable. We left the church in silence and hurried back to the relative safety of the apartment. Once there, Mother again made a great effort to be cheerful. She brewed us a hot cup of cocoa before handing me my presents. The first was a switchblade, with an intricate hand carved eagle's head on its wooden handle. I was sure it had been picked out by Father, whose favourite bird was the eagle. The mightiest of predators in his opinion. The second gift was a small but thick, leather bound blank notebook.

"A diary," Mother explained. "We are living through such turbulent times. I thought you might like to keep track of your thoughts and feelings. It might help. Later, you know." Her voice broke and I knew she was choking back tears. Weeks afterwards, when I recalled her words, I wondered if she had had a premonition of what was to come.

At the moment, I was grateful for the gifts. Grateful that despite the turbulence of our lives, my parents made the effort to show their love for me. And once again I recalled Brother Ferenc's advice to focus on what was good about my parents, instead of the bad. I threw my arms around Mother's shoulders and said a heartfelt thank you.

Two days later, on December 26th we learned that Soviet troops had surrounded Budapest, cutting off all access points in or out of the city. We were under siege!

Chapter 41

Wednesday, Jan. 12

"Medic! Help! I need a medic!" I yelled. My voice was not sufficient to rise above the din of wounded people crying out in pain, the blow of hammers and shovels against stone, the sirens and the numerous other sounds that followed in the wake of a bomb attack.

It was near the beginning of the third week of the siege. All the schools were now temporarily closed and I was out on a rescue mission with my local Levente group. While the majority of Levente groups were teamed with Nazi and Arrow Cross troops and were now often actively engaged in fighting, a few, like the one Tibor and I were a part of, helped with rescue efforts following the nightly air raids.

"Sissies!" Zoltan sneered whenever our paths crossed. Tibor and I didn't care. We were content with our assigned duties which comprised mostly of searching for injured people among the rubble of bombed buildings. We were both glad not having to fire a gun at anyone, either at the invading troops or at alleged traitors of the regime. Instead, we were involved with saving lives. It was a task that gave me an idea of how I could finally involve Judit in helping others.

"Tibor has a cousin who works with the female counterpart of the Levente group," I explained to her on my next visit to the safe house. I had first sought out Mrs. Varga to give her the small box of 'treasures' as she called them and then I hurried off to find Judit and tell her my plan.

"Tibor has already talked to his cousin and she is happy to give you her outgrown uniform. I have it right here." I shoved the bag at my feet toward hers. "I think it should fit you just fine and no one would think of questioning your identity while you're wearing it. But even if they do, you have your false papers now saying that you're Catholic. You can go to the bombed buildings like we do, and help search for trapped or injured people."

"But its Jewish people I want to help," she said. "They're the ones who are being arrested and killed." I looked at her, surprised.

"Don't you want to help anyone who needs it?" I asked. "Yes, it's the Jews who are being persecuted and they need protection, they need our help the most, but so do the people who are injured because of the bombing. They need to be found and taken to hospitals or given some emergency care right there. I thought you would want to help them too. There are often children among the injured. They're not responsible for what is happening. They're just frightened and hurt. Besides," I added as the thought occurred to me, "there could be Jews among the injured. Jews who may have been hidden by someone and would not want to be taken to a regular hospital. And what if a building with a Jewish star on it gets bombed? I don't know if many in the Levente group would rush to their aid." Judit looked down at her hands clasped together in front of her.

"You're right," she said after a few moments of silence. "I'm sorry. I shouldn't care who it is I'm helping if the person is hurt. And you're also right that there may be Jews among the injured. I'll do it," she nodded. "I'll join you and Tibor."

"No, you won't be joining us," I said, shaking my head. "You can't just come along. It's not done like that. I mentioned my idea to Brother Ferenc and he gave me the name of a group of nuns who are nurses. They go to the bombed sites to treat people. Some of the girls go with them. Here's the name of one of the nuns," I handed Judit a piece of paper. "She and her order are trying to secretly help Jews as well. Especially children. When you go to a bombed site, ask for her. All the nuns in her order have a weird looking head-dress that look like they have white wings coming out the side. They should be easy to spot. If you happen to find any injured Jews, they will look after them."

"Thank you," Judit said. "I'm sorry that I didn't want to do this at first. But, yes, this is good. I can't wait till the next air raid now! I've been feeling so frustrated at being inactive." She smiled, grabbed the bag at her feet and left.

Each day as I worked with the rescue effort, I was filled with conflicting emotions. I hated seeing the once stately buildings of Budapest destroyed and was sickened by the sight of so many people injured, bleeding, dying, or already dead. I cursed the Soviets for causing all this damage. At the same time, I was glad they were here, trying to vanquish the Nazis and Arrow Cross and put an end to their rule over our country. If only the Allied forces would hurry up and get the job done so that all this destruction could stop.

What would happen to Father, to our family when that happened, never entered my head.

I now ripped a frayed length of fabric from a small bundle I had in my uniform's pouch. I pressed it against the gaping wound in the thigh of the elderly man who lay pinned beneath a heavy iron beam.

"It's OK," I said, "help is on its way. You'll be fine" I knew that the help I claimed to be on its way might actually take a while to arrive. There were several people in more serious need of aid. But we had been instructed to keep any victims we found, calm.

"The more energy they exert in worry, the more blood and life they will lose," the nurse who gave us our hasty, basic training had instructed.

"Medic! Help!" I shouted again in frustration as the man's blood pulsed through the fabric, staining my fingers. I wished Judit was here. She would be better at coming up with comforting things to say. Our paths had only crossed a couple of times since she had started to help, but I had noticed her composed manner on those occasions and heard the soothing tone of her voice as she spoke with the injured victims. A sharp contrast to the panic I felt inside me with each person I found at the thought that they might die despite my efforts to help them.

At last, a nun who was also a nurse arrived.

"Good work!" she said smiling down at me. She bandaged the man's thigh properly, then turned to me. "Let's try and get this beam off of him, shall we?" She bent and grabbed hold of one end, while I hurried to the other, which I first had to free from beneath a pile of bricks and chunks of mortar. When she saw that I was ready, she gave a nod and we lifted. The man let out a loud moan as we eased the weight off his arms and chest. The beam was heavier than I had anticipated and I looked with surprise at the slight form of the nun who, though panting under the load, kept her end up as we eased it back to the ground a couple of meters away. She then returned to the man, running her fingers lightly over the now exposed area.

"I'm afraid he has a few broken ribs, and perhaps a fractured right arm as well. We're going to need a stretcher to move him. Can you stay with him a while longer?"

"Yes, certainly," I nodded. Now that the man was more comfortable and his open wound properly attended to, I was glad to have a few extra minutes of rest. Due to the fighting in the streets and the air raids, I had spent the previous night at the nearby Levente centre. Since dawn I had been digging through one destroyed building after another for survivors. The chance to just sit for a while was welcome.

The nun took off her black cape and laid it over the man. "I can do without this for the few minutes that I'm gone," she said, "and he needs to be kept warm. I'll try to bring a blanket back with me." With that she turned and picked her way over the debris to the Red Cross truck that was waiting at the side of the road. As I looked after her, admiring her kindness, I noticed Tibor emerge from a broken doorway, carrying a young boy piggyback style. A woman who I assumed was the boy's mother followed, holding a handkerchief to her forehead. Tibor's face was streaked with dirt and his teeth shone white in contrast as he smiled upon seeing me. I waved, then turned my attention back to the man lying prone next to me. I took the hand of his good arm between mine and tried to massage some warmth into his icy fingers.

"Do you have other family here?" I asked both in an attempt at conversation but also to determine if there was anyone to accompany this man to the makeshift hospital set up on the old market grounds. His eyes flickered open and he slowly shook his head.

"Son in war," he gasped. "Wife dead. Grandson,…" a tear trickled down his cheek and he again closed his eyes and turned his head away. A minute later the nun returned with the promised stretcher and blanket as well as a young medic who helped to transfer the old man carefully from the ground onto the stretcher. Together they carried him off and I was left to resume my hunt for other survivors, wondering about the untold story of his grandson.

By midafternoon we had scoured the area allotted to my group and our unit commander ordered us to return home to get some rest before reporting back early the next morning. I dragged my feet as I made my way along the snow-covered sidewalk looking forward to whatever food Mother had scraped together for me and then falling into a blissful sleep on my own bed.

I rounded the last corner onto our street and stopped, rooted to the ground. Most of the apartment building I had lived in my whole life was gone!

Chapter 42

A couple of the walls of the building were still standing, with the courtyard exposed and several of the apartments intact; but the rest was a pile of rubble. Parts of windows, tables, a mattress stuck out haphazardly. But most of the debris was unrecognizable.

Mother! Was she all right? Had she been safe in the shelter below ground? My fatigue vanished instantly, and I started running towards what used to be the building's front door. It was then that I noticed a shape emerge from the shadow of one of the remaining walls. It was that of a woman, wearing a long navy-blue coat and hat just like Mother's. My heart lurched with relief as we hurried towards each other and embraced.

"Thank goodness we were all in the bomb shelter. Miraculously no one was killed or injured," she explained as soon as we pulled apart. "The others have all left to go to a temporary centre for displaced people, but I couldn't leave. Not without letting you know that I was all right and telling you where I was. Come," she said looking me up and down, "you must be tired and famished. Let's go and get you something to eat. There is nothing left here for us." With that she put her arm around my shoulder and turned me towards the direction I had just come from.

As we walked away, I looked once more at the ruin of the building that had held my past. There was no hope of going back. Our side was completely destroyed. Life as I had known it was changed forever.

"I never thought about what it must be like to lose everything you own," I told Tibor when we met the next day at yet another bombed site. "When we come to these places I only pay attention to the physical injuries of the people we pull from the ruins. At least I used to. I never gave much thought to how each person felt about the destruction of their homes. I didn't realize how that too, can be a cause of great pain. Pain that is not visible on the outside."

"No, I hadn't thought about that either," Tibor replied, then paused in mid stride and looked at me. "This pain of losing your home, what's it like? I mean, do you actually hurt somewhere? Are you still able to help out here?"

"It's hard to describe," I said, looking down and kicking at a stone in our path. "I never thought about how our possessions shape who we are. Because of the feel of our home, the things I owned and loved, I thought of myself a certain way. It's like, they were the physical proof of what was important to me. Without my soccer ball, my bike, the pictures on my walls, the books I had read and owned, I feel kind of lost. There's a tightness in my gut because of the uncertainty of not having a home – of not having anything that's mine anymore. I, I feel sort of light headed, unfocused. Like, do I want all that stuff back or can I now become someone different? I won't be able to reach for the same old things when I want something to do. What will I choose to replace them with?" I looked up at Tibor. "Do you understand? Does it make any sense?" I asked.

"I don't know," he said. "Like you, I hadn't thought about what it must be like to lose everything you owned. I only thought about what it must be like to lose someone you loved. To lose your father." I felt a pang of guilt at his words.

"Of course," I said, laying a hand on Tibor's arm. "I'm sorry. Of course, that is so much more horrible than losing material things. I – I just hadn't realized what any of it must be like till now. I'm sorry that I hadn't thought of asking how you feel now without your father's presence. I was only concerned about your physical wellbeing, and you had assured me that you and your mother were doing fine."

"It's alright," Tibor said. "I probably wouldn't have thought of asking either. But yes, it's difficult without Father. I have this horrible longing for him all the time. Sort of like I'm always hungry. Mother is trying so hard to make up for his absence but that almost makes it worse. And I know we both worry about him, but we don't talk about it. It's too scary to wonder out loud if he's still alive." Tears filled Tibor's eyes at those last words. I laid my arms around his shoulders, not knowing what I could say that would be of comfort.

"But then I think of the Jews," Tibor said after a moment. "So many of them have lost everything.

Both their homes and families. I wonder how they can stand it."

"Like Judit," I agreed. "Yet she hasn't complained. Instead, she and the Vargas are focused now on helping others. They are looking after all those children and Judit is out at these ruins trying to do more. I suppose it helps them not to think about their own losses all the time."

"Yes," Tibor smiled through his tears. "That's probably good advice for us. Let's get to work!" He took off at a run and I followed.

Chapter 43

Friday, Jan. 12

Mother and I didn't stay at the homeless shelter for long.

"I'm so glad that your father was able to pull some strings and get us this apartment so quickly," Mother said as she walked from the kitchen to the living room and into the bedroom. "I know how busy he is these days. We haven't seen him in well over a week."

She was right. With the siege and constant fighting Father had been absent from home. Yet he had learned about the bombing of our building and had sent an Arrow Cross messenger to the makeshift displaced persons centre to let us know about the availability of this apartment on the Pest side of the river. Again, I thought of Brother Ferenc's advice. In the midst of this war Father still kept track of what was happening with us and looked out for our wellbeing. I was grateful for that. I hadn't liked staying at the shelter where there was absolutely no privacy.

"Do you think that this place used to belong to a Jewish family?" I asked, running my fingers over the rich, brown wood of the dining room table. It was set with four shiny porcelain plates and silver cutlery. "It looks like whoever left here, left in a hurry. Expecting to be back for supper."

"Probably," Mother replied. "It's on the edge of what had once been a predominantly Jewish quarter. Why? Does that bother you?" She asked.

"Well," I hesitated, wondering if Mother might express more sympathy towards the Jews when Father wasn't around. "What if the previous occupants are in a concentration camp right now? Or maybe they've been executed along the shores of the Danube. What if we're taking advantage of someone else's misfortune?" Mother hurried over to me, grasped my arms with her hands and looked me directly in the eyes.

"Listen to me," she said, her voice firm. "They were Jews. They are getting whatever they deserve. We needed someplace to live, and this was available. There is nothing to feel bad about. We've been through a lot in the past few weeks, but it can't last much longer like this. Just pray that things turn out alright for Father and us." She pulled me close and hugged me. "We have to be strong for one another. And though Father got this place for us, I haven't talked directly with him for almost two weeks. We must pray that everything is alright with him."

"Of course," I said, hugging her back. "I'm sorry. I don't want to add to your worries." I was sorry, but my sorrow was over realizing that Mother would never understand how I felt. She was too united in heart and mind with Father. I would have to continue to keep all my thoughts and feelings to myself.

Here, on the Pest side of the Danube, I didn't even have Tibor to talk with. The Levente chapter that we both belonged to, was too far from me now. With many of the streets in ruins between us and the danger of ongoing combat, I could no longer report for assignments in our old district.

"Let's see what else is left in this apartment," Mother said in a more cheerful tone. "We might even find some food if we're lucky."

Most of the previous occupant's furniture was still in the apartment but there were barren, lighter spots on the papered walls where pictures must have hung. An antique cabinet's glass doors stood open exposing its empty, raided interior. A large bookshelf in one corner had many gaps where a selective reader must have lifted only those books he was interested in reading. A few books lay scattered on the floor. I bent to pick one up. To my surprise, it was The Jungle Book, the story over which Jakob and I had cemented our friendship many years ago. I was flooded with grief as the enormity of everything I had lost washed over me anew. If only at the end of all this Jakob would return! Perhaps then it would be easier to make a fresh start.

The wardrobes in the bedrooms still held an assortment of clothing and in one I found pants, shirts and sweaters that were only slightly too large for me. Though I felt uncomfortable putting on someone else's clothes, it was better than staying in the Levente uniform that I had worn for the past three days.

Once I had changed and we were more or less settled in the apartment I persuaded Mother to let me leave and scavenge for some food. The kitchen cupboards were completely bare of anything edible except for one very stale loaf of bread.

Because of the siege our special food ration privileges had completely stopped. No fresh produce could enter the city and as the stores ran out of supplies, people were reduced to eating just about anything they could digest. The most popular commodity was the flesh of horses and donkeys that had been killed in the fighting and whose corpses lay abandoned in the streets. However, as arguments frequently broke out over their remains, I decided to try my luck elsewhere.

Before I left, I had pounded the stale loaf of bread till I had a large handful of dry crumbs. I put these together with a length of string that I had unraveled from a sweater into my pants pocket and headed to the nearest park. Once there, I made a small noose at one end of the string and laid it on the ground. I sprinkled some of the crumbs around it and then let out the rest of the string till it stretched to a nearby bench. I sat down and waited. Soon enough, the pigeons arrived, cooing and bobbing their heads up and down as they pecked at the crumbs. I sat and watched intently. When one of the pigeons stepped into the noose I gave a quick jerk on the string. It took five attempts before the noose tightened around a pigeon's thin leg. I reeled in my prey. I picked the frightened bird up and squeezing my eyes shut, I gave a swift twist to its neck. It lay limp in my lap. "I'm sorry," I whispered. I laid it gently on the bench, then went to repeat the process.

By the end of an hour, I had four birds. On the way back to our new apartment I traded one of the pigeons for a carrot and a potato. Mother was delighted with my catch and we feasted on it by candlelight.

It turned out that Mother was right. The siege did not last much longer.

Two days after our move to the apartment the Nazis admitted that they were losing the fight over Budapest and began their retreat.

On January 14th they blew up the Horthy Bridge, the southernmost bridge spanning the Danube. They destroyed the Ferenc Jozsef Bridge two days after that.

The following night, January 17th Mother and I sat by candlelight, each of us reading one of the abandoned books from the shelf, trying to ignore the noise of artillery fire and explosions that sounded very close to our building. There was no available shelter in the basement of our building. We figured it was safer to take our chances staying put than to risk being hit by stray bullets in the streets as we hurried to the nearest underground shelter.

Our reading was suddenly interrupted by the sound of hurried footsteps on the stairs and rapid, loud banging on our front door. It rose above the rumble of the streets. Mother jumped up and gripped my shoulder.

"Stay put and don't say a word!" she hissed before going to the door. She placed her hand on the handle and leaned against the door intending to open it just a crack to see who was on the other side. But as soon as the latch was released, the door was forcefully pushed open almost throwing Mother off balance. To my surprise, it was Father who stood there.

I had not seen Father in weeks, and I was shocked at the transformation in him. His always clean, crisp uniform was crumpled and stained. It hung loose around his shoulders. He must have gone as hungry as we had over the past few weeks.

His hair needed a trim and the stubble on his chin showed that he hadn't shaved in days. But it was the change in his eyes that struck me the most. Their once piercing, cold arrogance had been replaced by a look of fear and defeat. They darted here and there around the room in panic.

"Hurry!" Father commanded in place of a greeting. "We must leave at once! The Nazis are retreating. We must go with them. It's our only hope of staying alive."

Chapter 44

Ignoring his words and oblivious to his appearance, Mother threw her arms around him.

"Tomas, I am so glad to see you at last," she said, leaning her head against his chest. "Now everything will be alright."

"No. You don't understand," He said. He pushed her away and gripped her shoulders. "We're losing the battle against the Russians. The German army is retreating to Buda and then out of the city. By the morning they will have destroyed the last two bridges in order to stop the Russian infantry from pursuing them. This is our last chance to leave with the Germans. If I stay here the Russians will execute me as they are doing with the other Arrow Cross soldiers they capture. And who knows what they will do with you. This is our only chance to get away together. We must leave now!"

"Yes," Mother said. "We are ready to go. We lost everything in the bombing," she shrugged. "There's nothing to keep us here now. All I want is to be safe and to be together again." They both looked towards me expecting me to agree.

I was both elated and dismayed at Father's words. The Russians were winning! They were driving the Nazis and Arrow Cross from the country. Soon, very soon it seemed, we would be liberated! The fighting and bombing and the senseless killing would stop. Peace would return. Everyone, including the Jews would be able to walk freely in the streets again. Finally, it was happening!

But Father was demanding that we leave with the Nazis. With people who would try to continue their murderous mission elsewhere. I felt sick at the thought of going with them. I hated the beliefs of the Nazis and I did not want to live in a country that held them.

But If I didn't go, it would mean living without Father or Mother. My family.

I thought of the Vargas, Aunt Mimi, Judit and all the children whose parents had been torn from them against their will. Together, supporting each other, they were coping. But they also lived with the hope that one day their families would be reunited. If I refused to go with Mother and Father now, was there hope for me to ever see them again?

And how would they feel, abandoned by me, their only child? Could I do that to them?

Then I recalled the line of people, men, women, and children, stretching along the banks of the Danube, awaiting their execution. Dying for no other reason than being who they were born to be. Executed by men under my father's command. I thought of Tibor's father hauled off to the camps and of Jakob's eyes, filled with loathing when he looked at me for the last time. I wanted to be here when he returned. I wanted to explain.

The thoughts and images tumbled through my mind in mere seconds. I felt torn in two.

Father's eyes were boring into mine, willing me to obey. I leaned towards him and reached out my hand.

But my feet remained rooted to the floor. I could not move.

Brother Ferenc's words from the beginning of the school year popped into my mind. *"When you were a child, your parents made decisions for you. Now when you are confirmed, the choice will be yours."* He had been talking about more than just our religious formation. What he said applied to all aspects of life. I knew that now.

My body trembled. My outstretched arm dropped to my side. I took a step back, away from Father.

"I'm not going," I said.

Chapter 45

"What do you mean, you're not coming?" Father demanded after a moment of stunned silence. "Didn't you hear what I just said? We're losing! Our lives are in danger! It's our last chance to leave with the Germans before they blow up the last two bridges. Sergeant Molnar, your friend Zoltan's father is waiting with him in a car downstairs. All the troops are pulling out overnight. We must get away while we can! The Russians are going to be merciless with any Nazis or Arrow Cross they come upon."

"Zoltan is not my friend!" I said, my voice raised, almost shouting. "He never was. And I – I don't agree with what you, – with what the Arrow Cross and the Nazis are doing. It's wrong!" I tried to hold my gaze steadily on Father, ignoring the shocked expression on Mother's face at my words, at my attitude. "I don't know why you don't see that. The Jews, the Gypsies and everyone else you've been killing and sending off to those camps, they're all people just like us. They have a right to live as we do. I don't want to go and live among people who don't see that. I can't. I'm staying."

"What are you saying?" Father hissed. "You don't know what you're talking about! You will do exactly as I say! How dare you disobey me?" He grabbed the front of my shirt in his fist, yanking me closer to himself. "How dare you question my views? My judgement? All these days," he shoved me back and spread his arms wide, "I've been working, fighting to make life better for you and your mother, to create a world where only the best of humanity will live. I've been ridding the country of the vermin that has polluted it for years. We might be forced to leave now, but we will re-assemble, gather our forces and return strong and victorious! Now let's go! I'll deal with your arrogance later."

"No! I'm not going! I'm staying here where I can be of help. You can't make me go with you!" I pulled myself up straighter, squared my shoulders, hoping Father would see that I was now as strong as he was, if not stronger. I glanced at the pistol at his side. "You'll have to shoot me first." I added, hoping I sounded braver than I felt.

"You thought the Vargas were fine people until you discovered they were Jewish," I carried on, still hoping to change Father's mind. "Then all of a sudden you hated them. Only because of their religion. But they are still the same. The same good people. They are not vermin. Hendrik, or Jakob, is still my friend whether he is Jewish or not. It makes no difference. It's who he is as a person that counts."

"Well, I highly doubt he's still your friend," Father sneered. "The last I heard the Nazis had lost track of him. It can only mean one thing. He's dead."

Father's words sent a chill down my spine. I almost lost my resolve. The hope of Jakob's return had sustained me over the past months.

"You can't know that," I said, unable to control the sudden tremor in my voice. "Maybe he escaped and is on his way back. You and the Nazis are leaving just in time. Jakob will return to a country that is free." My words renewed my courage and I clung to them, willing myself to believe their truth.

"Yes, we are leaving just in time," Father replied, "but not because of your idiotic fabrication. I told you, the Russians will kill me together with you, your mother and all of us belonging to the Arrow Cross if they find us here. Now come on! Stop wasting time. Get moving!"

"They won't kill me," I said, not budging. I took a deep breath and continued. "I don't belong to the Arrow Cross. Not really. Not like you. I haven't for a long time – not since that day in the ghetto when I saw what was really happening." I tore at the shirt of the Levente uniform as I spoke, popping the buttons, ripping it off my shoulders. I had reluctantly put it on again that morning for protection before I went out into the streets. I threw the shirt on the floor between us. "Ever since that day, I've been working behind your back for the other side. Helping to hide Jews so they wouldn't be captured by you. I was the one who helped the Vargas escape. They and many others will speak up in my defense, should that be necessary. So no, I'm not worried that the Russians will kill me."

"What are you saying?" Father said, lunging towards me again. "The Vargas? You helped them? You are my son! How could you – how dare you work against me?" Mother laid a restraining hand on his arm.

"Ivan," she pleaded with me. "Please listen to your father. You are still a child. You don't understand. Your father knows what he's talking about. You can't stay behind. How can you possibly think that you could do that? How can you think of leaving us? Who will look after you?"

Father ignored her as if she hadn't spoken. His eyes filled with rage. He took a step towards me. He slapped me hard across the face. He raised his arm to hit me again. This time his hand was clenched in a tight fist.

"Tomas," Mother cried. "Don't!"

"I worked against you because you are wrong," I said, also balling my hands into fists, but restrained myself from striking back. "Please, can't you see that?" I no longer cared about the tremble in my voice or the tears that coursed down my cheeks. "I love you. You're my father. But I can't go along with what you and the Arrow Cross and the Nazis are doing to the Jews and others. Please," I repeated, "it's not too late for you to reconsider. We can stay here together. I can make sure we are all protected."

I didn't know if I could carry through with that promise, but it might get Father and Mother to stay. And once Father convinced the Russians that he had a change of heart surely they wouldn't hurt him.

Father and I stared at one another, neither of us giving way.

Our deadlock was shattered by the sound of the building's main doors opening below. We heard heavy footsteps ascending the stairs.

"Molnar!" Father hissed, glancing behind him. "He must have grown impatient. He's coming up! If he discovers what you have been doing, he'll kill you on the spot. That's what we do with a traitor."

I knew that what Father said was right. Sergeant Molnar wouldn't waste time discussing the rightness or wrongness of the Arrow Cross. He would take immediate action.

My heart pounded in my chest. What had I done? What was about to happen to me? If Father wouldn't stay here with Mother, at least I didn't want to part with them in anger.

"Remember what you told Tibor?" I said quietly, composing myself. "When he came to see you about his father? You said that he is a man now, capable of making his own choices. Well, I too have made my own choices. I'm making my choice now. Please try to understand."

Another moment of silence stretched between us, penetrated only by the sound of footsteps drawing closer.

Father sighed. His shoulders sagged beneath his loose shirt in resignation. Before I could do anything, he reached out, grabbed my arm and shoved me into the large, half empty wardrobe that stood open behind me. He retrieved my shirt from the floor, threw it in after me and slammed the doors shut. "Don't make a sound!" he ordered. I saw Mother's hand cover her mouth in horror just before darkness enveloped me.

I crouched in the corner of the wardrobe in stunned silence, hugging my knees against my chest. What had just happened? What was Father doing?

Within seconds I heard Sergeant Molnar's voice in the room.

"What's going on? Why is this taking so long? We have to leave!" Had Zoltan followed him, I wondered?

"It's that son of mine," Father replied. "Apparently he's gone out on some foolish errand and Ilonka doesn't want to leave without him. But I agree, we can't wait any longer. Ivan is a resourceful lad. He can look after himself until we return. And he has friends to help him out. I'm sure he'll be fine."

"Tomas! What are you saying?" Mother's shrill voice objected. "We can't leave without Ivan. We can't leave him behind. We have to stay!"

"Ilonka! Pull yourself together!" Father ordered. "You know this is how it must be for now. Ivan's very capable. He'll understand. And hopefully it won't be for long. Now let's go." I heard shuffling and Mother's muffled protests as they moved towards the door. Their steps retreated out into the corridor of the courtyard and receded down its length. Then I heard Father's voice again.

"Hold on to Ilonka for a minute, Molnar, and carry on! I – I forgot something."

Footsteps hurried back towards me. I heard Father re-enter the room. He came straight to the wardrobe. There was a light thump near the top of the door. I pictured Father's forehead resting against it.

"Ivan, I'm sorry things turned out this way," he whispered. "I, I guess you did what you had to do. But once this is all over, I will come back for you." There was a brief pause. I knew he was hoping for a response from me, but I didn't know what to say. Besides I doubted that any sound would get past the lump in my throat. "I'm sorry it has to end this way." Father continued, "I love you too, son."

The lump in my throat grew even larger at those words. I realized that it was the first time that I heard my father say openly that he loved me. I fought the urge to burst through the wardrobe doors, throw my arms around his neck and agree to go with them. I forced myself instead to focus on what the Arrow Cross and Nazis stood for. What I would be a part of if I were to leave. I remained silent and immobile in the darkness.

A moment later I once again heard Father's steps recede out of the room. Though he had said that he would come back for me I sensed that I would never see him again. I bowed my head onto my knees and wept.

Chapter 46

Jan. 18, 1945

I stayed huddled in the wardrobe for a long time. Not because I thought I faced any danger in coming out. It was clear that Father and Mother had left with Sergeant Molnar and Zoltan and I wasn't scared of the advancing Russian troops. Even if they were to find me still wearing my Levente uniform I was sure that I could explain everything and call on the Vargas and others at the safe house to vouch for me. All of them would be free now.

No, I was simply too shocked at what had just transpired and the dramatic turn my life had taken once again. I had tried to sound confident when confronting Father, but I wondered what I was going to do now.

I must have dozed off, for suddenly I was roused by a loud explosion that shook the entire building. Within minutes it was followed by another. It took me a while to remember where I was, what had happened. I stretched my stiff limbs and pushed my way cautiously out of the wardrobe.

The room had no lights on, yet it was lit by an eerie, flickering, orange glow. Mesmerized, I went to the window that faced towards the Danube. Silhouettes of ruined buildings and trees blocked my view of the river, but the source of the light was clearly there. Recalling Father's words from earlier on I realized that what he had foretold, was happening. The last two bridges spanning the Danube had been destroyed. Pest was completely cut off from Buda. I was cut off from my old friends, my school, Brother Ferenc and Mr. Wallenberg at the Swedish Embassy.

I stood transfixed by the sight and what it signified. One part of my vague plan had been to seek the advice of Brother Ferenc, maybe even stay at the monastery for a while if he could arrange that. That was no longer possible. The only people I knew on the Pest side were the Vargas and the other people hiding with them at the safe house.

Had they survived? It seemed like a long time ago since I last saw any of them.

It had been easy to say to Father that I had everything under control and that I would be protected. But really, what did I know? Who would be willing to take me in? To look after me? And now that the Russians had taken control of Pest, what would happen to its Hungarian citizens? Would the Russians prove to be just a different set of invaders or were they truly our saviours? I knew that only time would tell.

I still had this apartment, I reasoned, and could probably stay here until someone came back to lay claim to it or until the new people in power decided that they had a better use for it. I suspected that with all the bombed buildings there would be quite a shortage in housing. I was confident that as long as I had a place to live, I could take care of myself.

I walked over to the coal stove and lit a fire under the remains of the pigeon stew Mother had made. There were only a couple of pieces of meat left floating together with a small chunk of potato. Though it was unappetizing, I eagerly gobbled it down. I was always hungry these days and had stopped being squeamish about what I ate. At least we hadn't starved like so many others during the siege.

It was eventually my unsatisfied hunger that drove me to change into regular civilian clothes and venture out into the street. It was mid-morning by now, and I squinted against the weak rays of the sun that peeked out from gathering snow clouds. Even after the months of destruction and violence that I had witnessed, the sight that now met my eyes was devastating. Rubble and dead bodies littered the streets. Plumes of thick smoke rose all along the river while the sounds of continued fighting drifted over from Buda.

All thoughts of finding food deserted me.

As I picked my way along, I dared not look too closely at the bodies. From the uniforms I could tell that they were mostly Arrow Cross and Nazi soldiers with some civilians scattered among them. Did Father and Mother make it across the river? Surely, they had left in time? Would I ever find out what became of them?

Without intentionally planning to, I found myself making my way towards the safe house where the Vargas and Judit were staying. The streets, or what remained of them, were still occupied by soldiers but they were now clearly Russian or a part of the Hungarian army that was distinct from the Arrow Cross. They were too busy looking for remnants of the defeated forces to pay much attention to me.

It was only as I neared the destroyed pillars of Margit Bridge that I realized that I was only a few blocks from the safe building. I was shocked to suddenly hear my name called.

"Ivan! Ivan! Over here!" Judit's familiar voice sent a thrill through my body. I turned my head this way and that, squinting through the smoky haze and the now gently falling snow, searching. I spotted her standing on top of a pile of rubble, madly waving her arm. I waved back and we ran towards each other, stumbling over boulders in our haste.

"Ivan! I'm so glad you're alive!" she said throwing her arms around me, almost knocking me over. "I could tell it was you right away from the way you walked, despite that oversized jacket," she laughed, stepping back as if to get a better look at me. "We were so worried about what might have happened to you during last night's fighting and retreat. We thought you might be stuck on the other side of the river for a long time. The Vargas worry about you almost as much as they worry about their own son, Jakob."

"So, they are alright," I said, relieved.

"Yes. Them and Aunt Mimi and Lilly and all the children. All very hungry, but alive. Which is why I'm out here trying to find something to eat that I can take back for everyone. I've become the official scavenger," she said with a degree of pride in her voice. "But it's been a couple of days since I could get outside because of all the fighting so everyone is getting desperate for food."

"Yes, that's what brought me out here too," I said. "Though once I saw all this," I waved my arm at the scene before us, "I kind of forgot my hunger." Judit nodded her head in understanding, her mouth pulled into a grim line as we looked about us.

"How *have you* been doing?" she asked. "How did you get to this side of the river with the bridges gone?" I explained to her about our bombed building and how Father had found us an apartment over here on the Pest side.

"Your father," she said thoughtfully, "What is he doing now that the Russians have taken control?"

"My parents, they're, - they're gone," I said, not sure how to explain all that had happened. "They left with the Nazis when they retreated. Just before the last bridges were blown up. I – I chose to stay behind." Judit didn't seem surprised at my words. She understood.

"Do you think that things will ever go back to being normal again?" she asked after a moment of silence. Her eyes filled with tears. "Will we, will all those children ever see our parents again?"

"I don't know," I shook my head, unable to imagine how it was possible to rebuild after so much destruction. To rebuild both the buildings and our lives.

As we stood there, silently contemplating our fate, a Russian soldier came over and said something unintelligible to us. I shook my head and gestured that we had no idea what he was saying. He then opened his mouth, pointed into it and then pointed down the length of rubble towards an army truck that was parked along an unobstructed stretch of road.

"Food!" I cried, suddenly understanding. "He's telling us that we can get food there. Come on!" I grabbed Judit's hand and after saying a hasty thank you to the soldier, we took off.

Sure enough, from the back of the truck, Russian soldiers were handing out bags of flour, powdered milk, jugs of water and even small coils of sausage to the hollow-cheeked survivors that stood about with their arms outstretched.

"This is way better than pigeon stew," I said, smiling as we headed back to the safe house, our arms loaded with supplies.

Chapter 47

Feb. – May

Gradually, over the next few weeks Pest came back to life. The fighting still raged on the Buda side of the river until February 11th when the Nazis and remaining Arrow Cross finally withdrew from Gellert Mountain, their last stronghold.

When I heard the reports of the Nazi retreat, I wondered about the fate of my parents. I knew the fighting in Buda had been intense and thousands of escaping soldiers had been killed. Were my parents among them or had they managed to survive? Or had my Father, like many other Hungarian soldiers, suddenly changed his mind and defected to the other side and was now fighting with the Soviet army? Would I ever find out?

I didn't have much time to dwell on such questions. Now that the fighting was over in

Budapest, everyone was anxious to piece their lives back together regardless of how fractured they had become. While most of the Soviet soldiers were helpful, many others resorted to looting and harassing the local citizens. People suspected of having collaborated with the Germans were arrested and shipped off to Soviet labour camps. We had been freed from one kind of oppression, but we still couldn't feel safe.

"You must stay with us now," Mr. and Mrs. Varga had insisted that first day when Judit and I returned to their apartment with our cache of food, and I told them of my refusal to leave with my parents. "We'll take care of you as long as you need or want to remain with us." I was grateful for their offer. It was what I had hoped for.

"Thank you," I responded. "But," I said, looking around me at their cluttered living room, "why don't you all move into the apartment where Mother and I stayed? There is so much more space there. I doubt anyone is going to worry about who lives where for a while."

It was a week before we sorted out the various living arrangements. Aunt Mimi and Lilly decided to remain at the safe house for the time being.

"This place will be plenty big enough for the two of us once all this extra bedding and furniture is gone. It will do us good to have our own place."

Judit, together with the rescued children, had arranged to stay at the orphanage run by the nuns whom she had assisted at the bombed sites. The Vargas had urged her to live with them as well.

"Thank you," she had hugged Mrs. Varga. "But I can't leave these children. I have promised their parents that I would look after them until they return or if that doesn't happen, until they can each be placed with a new family. They trust me and depend on me. I'm the only link they have to their past. We are like a family now. I can't leave them. Not yet."

I admired Judit's sense of responsibility and commitment. Life with the nuns at the orphanage, having to live under their rule, would be foreign and confining for her. Yet, I suspected that Judit would find ways of making life there as normal as possible for both herself and the children.

As their fear of persecution diminished, the Vargas tried to obtain information about Jakob. Offices opened in various parts of the city where people could go to inquire about surviving relatives. Because of the bombed streets, the ruined buildings and hosts of displaced people, there was much confusion.

Near the beginning of February, we heard on the radio that on January 27th, the Auschwitz concentration camp had been liberated by Soviet troops. After that day, newly discovered horrors of what went on in Auschwitz, and other 'death camps' as they were now commonly called, poured over the airwaves. Photographs in the newspapers of emaciated survivors were hard to look at especially with the gnawing fear that we might recognize Jakob as one of them. Yet, however difficult, Mr. and Mrs. Varga carefully examined each face in the hopes that they might have proof that Jakob was still alive. I hadn't told them about what Father had said before he left, about the Nazis losing track of Jakob. I didn't want to diminish their hope.

Daily, Mr. Varga made the rounds of various offices and agencies that had been set up, dedicated to finding and reuniting deported family members. He spent hours poring over lists pinned to the sides of buildings or on the round bulletin pillars at street corners, lists both of people who had returned and those who had perished. Each night he came back dejected, having learned nothing about Jakob's fate.

"It's as if he has disappeared off the face of the earth," he shook his head. "There are records saying he was sent to Auschwitz, but then nothing. Not even that he had died."

Mrs. Varga's tactic was more personal. Every morning she went to the railway station, waiting for trains to arrive that might be bringing back survivors from the concentration camps. She would question those passengers, regardless of which camp they had been prisoner at, about whether they had known someone called Hendrik Varga, or Jakob Kline or any combination of those two names. At the end of each day, she too came back disappointed.

Since the Vargas were preoccupied with finding Jakob and with Judit gone, it fell to me to procure food for our daily meals. Peasants began to trickle into the city selling their meagre wares and shop owners re-opened their stores selling or bartering the supplies that once again started to arrive daily.

Disheartened by the destruction of our beautiful city, I also joined up with a labour group assigned to remove corpses and clear away the rubble. Once that was done, we would assist in the re-building process. Though some schools that were still standing began to offer classes again we were also given the option of studying on our own and then writing a comprehensive test at the start of the next school year to see if we qualified to move into the next grade. Unable to return to the school run by the Franciscan brothers, and being too restless to sit still in a classroom all day when there was so much that needed doing, I chose this latter option.

For each day's work I was paid a small wage. After spending some of it on food and other necessary supplies for our household, I dutifully gave the remainder over to Mrs. Varga. However, on a sunny day in early April, when the Danube was finally free of ice floes, I took my earnings from the day and paid a fisherman to ferry me across to Buda. We landed near the base of Gellert Mountain and I made my way painstakingly up around the mountain side and over towards our old district. Though I had been working daily amidst the ruins of Pest, it was a shock to see the devastation that had taken place on the Buda side in the few months since I was last here. I arrived at the monastery gates just as the sun was disappearing behind the hills. I was heartened to see that at least within these walls, everything was as it had been. Brother Ferenc embraced me when he saw that it was I who had called on him.

"I am so very happy to see you, my son," he said. "I had feared for your life when the Soviets liberated the city and so many of the Arrow Cross and their families perished. But I should have known that you would manage to look after yourself despite the difficult position you were in." It was good to hear those words, to know that someone had that much faith in me. And to hear him call me 'son' at a time when I felt so fatherless.

We spent the next hour exchanging our diverse experiences. I learned that Tibor's father had returned near the beginning of March, weak and thin, and minus a couple of toes lost to frostbite, but otherwise whole. The family had gone to stay with Tibor's aunt in a nearby village until Tibor's father regained his strength and could return to work.

"Unfortunately, I have no news of Raoul Wallenberg," Brother Ferenc shook his head with dismay. "No one seems to have heard from him or seen him since the Soviets arrived in Budapest. There are many rumors flying about, and his aides are doing everything possible to locate him, but so far without success. It's impossible to think that a man who risked so much to save others might be in trouble and we are powerless to assist in any way."

"Yes." I said. "I'm sorry that now – now that's its him who might need to be rescued, I'm no longer able to get information that might help."

"Hmm." Brother Ferenc sat lost in thought for a moment, then said, "There's nothing that you or I can do to help Wallenberg, but there might be something you can do to help find Jakob."

I sat up straight and leaned close, eager to hear what he had to say. "The Nazis kept meticulous records of who they sent to the various camps and who they killed in each," Brother Ferenc explained. "It's mostly through the records that have been seized from them so far, that people are finding out about the fates of their loved ones. But not all the records are in the possession of the Allies yet. And even so, no system is perfect. Some people have managed to slip through the cracks.

"What if Jakob turns up one day, only to discover that the building you had lived in is in ruins. And he might believe that like him, his parents too had been captured. After all, he thinks that you had run off to do your Father's bidding that day back in the ghetto. He might not only not know how to find them, but he might assume that there's no point in looking. That they had died. What would he do? Where would he turn? How would he survive from day to day?"

"Do you think that he would come to you?" I asked. Brother Ferenc shook his head.

"Not necessarily. He must have experienced many horrific things in Auschwitz. He doesn't know my attitude towards Jews. He has no reason to trust in my support."

"So then, what can I do? What are you suggesting? How can *I* help?"

"Many people who have lost everything during the war are staying in makeshift shelters and getting their meals at the 'soup kitchens' set up by organizations such as the Red Cross. Perhaps you can volunteer at the various locations throughout the city. Who knows, Jakob might turn up at one of them."

It seemed like a long shot at the time, but eventually that is exactly how I found Jakob. But our meeting did not turn out to be the joyous reunion that I had anticipated.

Chapter 48

May, 1945

I had been helping out at soup kitchens for weeks, every few days moving from one location to another, then starting the circuit again. My hope that this might actually work in finding Jakob was beginning to waver. I no longer searched through the waiting line, eagerly anticipating seeing his familiar face. The job had become a tedious routine of ladling soup, or goulash or whatever was on the menu that day into one outstretched bowl after another. I barely glanced up at each face before they moved on and the next bowl was thrust at me.

And then, when I happened to look up at the next person in line on that May afternoon, my eyes locked with those of the young man in front of me. Instant recognition flared on his face, echoing the one that must have blossomed on mine.

Before I could react or say anything, Jakob was across the table. He barreled into me, knocked the bowl from my hand and splayed me flat on my back on the pavement. He straddled me and delivered blow after blow to my face and shoulders. Pain erupted in my head. Blood oozed from my nose.

Vaguely I was aware of people rushing towards us. I heard yelling. Hands reached out, grasped Jakob's arms, pulled him off me. Shocked, I staggered to my feet.

"What are you doing?" I shouted at Jakob. "Are you crazy? Don't you recognize me? Don't you know who I am? I'm Ivan, your friend. Why are you fighting me?" Though I was bruised and bleeding and hurting, it was the shock of his vicious attack that overwhelmed me.

"You are not my friend!" Jakob spit the words at me. "You're a traitor. You betrayed me. You destroyed my family. You sent me to the concentration camp. You are responsible for having my parents killed. I will make you pay. It's your turn to suffer now," he shouted, struggling to free himself from the grip of the men holding him.

"Hendrik, listen to me," I pleaded resorting to the name I had used when we were the best of friends. "Look at me. I am not who you think I am."

"I know who you are," he hissed. "You are a Nazi. And I am not Hendrik. My name is Jakob." He flailed again against the men's grasp, desperate to get at me again.

"Jakob, then," I readily agreed. "What does it matter? I'm still your friend. I never stopped being your friend."

"You are no friend of mine," he said. I flinched at the disgust in Jakob's voice. What had happened to him? Why was he acting and talking like this? Why did he say that I had killed his parents?

"A friend wouldn't have stood by and done nothing when I was taken captive and carted off to a concentration camp," he continued. "A friend wouldn't have gone to report my parents so that they too would be arrested. A friend wouldn't have caused my family to die." Jakob's voice trembled as he uttered those last words and tears trickled down his cheeks. A hush had fallen over the group surrounding us. I stood stunned by his words until slowly the truth dawned on me.

He didn't know! Brother Ferenc had been right. Jakob suspected nothing of what I had truly done.

Of course not. How could he?

Who would have told him what happened here while he was at the camp? The last thing he knew was my father's order commanding me to go and have the guards arrest his parents. He had seen me turn and apparently hurry off to do Father's bidding. He couldn't have known that instead of obeying Father, I had chosen to help.

All this time, he had thought that I had betrayed our friendship, my loyalty to him and his family. If that was the case, he had the right to hate me. I had to correct his misconception.

"I did not cause your family to die," I said, looking him straight in the eyes. "They are alive. Your parents, your aunt Mimi and cousin Lilly, even your housekeeper, are all alive. I helped to save their lives."

Jakob's eyes widened at my words, incredulous. *'Alive? Because of you?'* He whispered the words. The colour drained from his face and his body went limp.

"You're lying," he said out loud, but this time his words lacked the force of conviction. I motioned to the men to release him.

"It's true," I said. "I will take you to them. But first, come," I reached towards Jakob and wrapped my arm around his back, surprised at how thin he felt. With my other hand I pulled a handkerchief from my pocket and held it to my bleeding nose. "There's a coffee shop across the street that's open," I said, my voice muffled by the cloth. "We can go there and talk. I'll explain everything and you can tell me what happened with you."

The supervisor overseeing the volunteers, readily excused me from my post. Jakob had gone limp and as if in a daze, he allowed me to guide him along the sidewalk, past the people in line and across the street to the coffee shop. Except for giving our orders, we remained silent until the waitress, who was trying hard not to react to my beat-up face, placed our coffees in front of us and left. Jakob still seemed suspicious. He sat stiffly in his chair and his face was like a mask, revealing nothing of how he felt. Had he learned such self-control in the camp? Was that one of the tactics of survival?

I too was nervous now, after Jakob's unexpected fury. I twisted the handkerchief this way and that, dabbing at my nose, though the flow of blood had stopped. Would Jakob believe me? I wondered. Would he understand that I had done what I thought would help him and his family the most? I still didn't know how, what I had done, had failed to help him. When the rest of his family was saved, his aunt and cousin rescued from the train, why did he end up in Auschwitz? I too wanted answers.

It was clear he wasn't going to be the one to speak first, so I cleared my throat and began.

"That day in the ghetto, I'm sorry that things happened the way they did. I wish it could all have been avoided, but everything happened so suddenly. There was so little time to think." I tried to explain how I had felt about what I witnessed in the ghetto that day, the realization of what the Arrow Cross and my father were really doing and the sure conviction that it was wrong. I told Jakob of my confusion at discovering that he was Jewish and assured him that for me it didn't change anything about my friendship for him.

"I didn't understand then why you hadn't told me, but I do now," I said. "I know your father forced you and your mother never to talk about your Jewish past. Your mother told me."

"My mother told you?" Jakob asked leaning towards me, his face suddenly animated. "When – when did she tell you?"

"I'm not sure," I said trying to remember. "About a week after you were captured. Once we had a chance to talk about all that had happened." Jakob's features softened at my words. He let out a sigh and his body slackened. He downed his coffee in a couple of gulps.

"So she really is alive!" He whispered, as if still trying to convince himself. He nodded at me to continue.

I told him about how I had decided not to follow Father's orders. I told him about the vague plan I concocted on my way back to the apartment. Of sneaking over to the monastery and seeking the advice of Brother Ferenc. Of his immediate willingness to help. Of convincing Jakob's parents that their lives were in danger and to follow me. About our escape through the tunnels and about Raul Wallenberg and his safe houses.

"So my parents really are alive? Jakob asked yet again.

"Yes, of course they are," I nodded. "They have a new apartment now. I will take you to them. They have been desperately trying to find out whether you are still alive. That's one of the reasons I've been helping at the soup kitchens, to try to find you. Every few days I go to a different location." Jakob slumped forward in his chair and buried his face in his hands.

"How could I have been so wrong about everything? About you?" he groaned. "I should never have doubted you." He looked up at me. "I'm so sorry for all the horrible things I thought about you. The whole time at the concentration camp I thought you had betrayed my family – that you were responsible for their deaths. I wanted revenge. All I wanted was to live long enough to return and pay you back for what you had done. Can you forgive me?" He again pressed his face into his hands. His shoulders shook. Tears leaked through his fingers.

"Of course, I forgive you," I said as tears flooded my own eyes. I reached out across the small table and grasped his hand. "But I too need forgiveness," I continued. "Before all of this, I know that I was the driving force behind all of our training. I wanted so much to join in the war. On the side of the Nazis and the Arrow Cross. I never really listened to your concerns." I took a deep breath. It was difficult to openly admit to my own mistakes. It was seeing the anguish in Jakob's eyes that gave me the strength to continue. "I willingly blinded myself to the truth. Because I wanted to fight. Because I wanted to be important and powerful like my father. I don't know what I would have done if you had told me back then that you were Jewish. It wasn't until that day in the ghetto that I could no longer deny what was really happening. So, I am sorry too. I'm sorry for all you had to suffer."

Jakob smiled at me through his tears. He reached across the table with his other hand and gripped my shoulder.

"I forgive you," he said.

It was as simple as that. Once again, we were friends. The best of friends!

Chapter 49

It was easy to talk after that. And to eat. Suddenly we were both famished. We ordered soup and crepes. Though Jakob was eager to see his parents, there was too much for the two of us to say to each other first.

"Tell me what happened with you," I said as we waited for the food to arrive. "Father told me you were sent to Auschwitz."

"Yes." Jakob rolled up his left sleeve and showed me the numbers 18036 tattooed on his forearm. "Everything was taken from us when we arrived there. Even our names. I became a number. Numbers don't need kindness or compassion. And very little food," he smiled wryly. "But I was fortunate to make a couple of friends there. One of them especially, taught me that even in a place like Auschwitz it's possible to remain human and keep our dignity."

He gazed off, lost in thought for a moment as I tried to imagine what he was alluding to. I realized then, that though we were once again the friends we had been in our childhood, our experiences over the past several months had changed both of us in ways that would take a long time to understand.

"You know, Wallenberg and his men tried to rescue you," I said. "They searched for your aunt and cousin as well. They were found, but you seemed to have vanished in the trains. Wallenberg had your Aunt Mimi and Lilly taken off the train, but the guards couldn't find you."

"Aunt Mimi and Lilly are alive too? You mentioned their names before. I – I don't understand, how that could be. I saw them with my own eyes as they were being forced to leave the train at gunpoint."

"No," I shook my head. "You must be mistaken." I told him then about how Mr. Wallenberg, at Brother Ferenc's insistence, discovered which train they were on and raced to intercept it in order to remove them. "They found your Aunt Mimi and Lilly but the guards insisted that they couldn't find you. They went from car to car shouting your name to no avail. They ended up having to leave without you."

Jakob stared at me wide eyed and clasped a hand over his mouth. Tears began streaming down his face again. I sat helpless, confused by his reaction.

"I can't believe it. It could all have been avoided," he choked out at last, lowering his hand. "All of it."

"I don't understand," I said. "What are you talking about?"

"The train. It was so packed. It was unbearable," Jakob gazed into the distance, remembering. "I was separated from Aunt Mimi and Lilly but I knew that they were on one of the other cars up ahead. I didn't care. I was glad not to be with them. I hated myself for my role in what happened in the ghetto. I felt responsible for Gabor's death. I was so ashamed. I just wanted to hide, to get away from everyone, but it was impossible.

"Eventually I squeezed myself into the back corner of the car. I huddled there for hours. There was a small knothole in one of the boards through which I could get a bit of fresh air and look out every once in a while. When the train stopped once, I noticed people being led off by armed guards. They were all shot. Their bodies were left bleeding on the snow when the train pulled away. It was horrible." Jakob shuddered and focused on me again.

"When the train stopped the next time, I saw Aunt Mimi and Lilly being led off the car ahead of mine at gunpoint. I was convinced that they were about to be killed. I couldn't bear it. I squeezed my eyes shut and clamped my hands over my ears. I didn't want to see or hear anything. I stayed that way till the train started moving again. Till I was convinced that we had left them well behind." Jakob took a deep breath and shook his head again. "But I hadn't been able to drown out all the sounds completely. I remember hearing muffled shouts, but I didn't pay attention. It must have been the guards calling my name. I could have gotten off. I could have gone with Aunt Mimi and Lilly. I could have avoided Auschwitz."

Jakob's body began to shake uncontrollably at the realization. I shifted my chair next to his and hugged him close.

"It's all right," I said softly. "It's all over now. You're safe, and soon you will see your family again." My words felt inadequate, but gradually Jakob's body calmed and he regained his composure. I gently released him and moved my chair back to the other side of the table. Our soup arrived.

"We were given soup at the camp," Jakob smiled after tasting his first mouthful, "but it was nothing like this." As we ate, he told me about his arrival at Auschwitz and all that happened with him there and afterwards. He told me of his daring escape and why the Nazis had lost track of him.

Chapter 50

Epilogue

It was dark by the time we left the café. We were on the Buda side of the Danube and as it was a mild May evening, after a short streetcar ride down the hillside, we walked along the ramparts towards the temporary pontoon bridge. All of a sudden, Jakob's steps slowed. He didn't seem so eager to meet his parents.

"Are you sure they will want to see me?" he asked numerous times. "They're not angry about what I did? That I revealed our identity as Jews? Are you sure Aunt Mimi and Lilly don't hate me for causing Gabor's death?" I had told him earlier that his aunt, cousin and their housekeeper were visiting his parents for the evening

"Yes!" and "No!" I stressed over and over again, but still his steps slowed even more the closer we got to the building. When we arrived, he climbed the stairs to our apartment like a mountain climber carrying a tremendous load on his back.

I was the one who knocked. Then I stepped to the side. The door opened and Mrs. Varga stood in the warm glow of the kitchen behind her.

"Ivan, we were beginning to worry about you," she started to say, wiping her hands on her apron. Then she looked up and saw who was standing in front of her. Her hands flew to her chest and she gasped. In the next instant, her arms were around Jakob. She laughed and cried at the same time.

"Janos, Mimi, Lilly, Magda!" she shouted. "Come! Come and see who has finally returned home!"

Within seconds everyone was gathered around Jakob. He needn't have had any fears. There was no blaming. No accusations. Just genuine joy and relief at his return. Chairs were pulled up, food laid on the table and all the various disturbing stories exchanged amidst tears and even some laughter.

Perhaps I should have left, gone to my room. After all, I was not really a part of this family. This was their moment to reunite. But they kept pulling me in, kept including me in all the recollections of their anecdotes, their thoughts, their affections - till I felt that I was woven into their lives in some essential way that could never be unraveled now.

Hours later, After Aunt Mimi, Magda and Lilly had left, and as Jakob and I headed towards the room that we were to share now as brothers, Mr. Varga stopped us.

"Jakob, look at you. You left as a boy and came back a man. Both of you," he said encompassing me with his gaze. "Both of you are men now. Men that I would be proud to know, no matter what our connection."

314

Acknowledgements

There are many people whom I would like to thank for helping me to bring this book to completion. My editors, Katherine, Paddy and Kristin; my enthusiastic first readers of the manuscript, Ted and Nancy, my husband Bruce for his formatting skills and Tim for the cover design. Also, there were the several Holocaust survivors whom I interviewed and who graciously shared their memories, both painful and triumphant. This story grew out of their collective remembrances.

And finally, I am grateful for my entire family who has been my pillar of support throughout all my writing. I could not have persevered without them.